Midnight Hunted

Mated By Midnight
Book 2

Heather Hildenbrand

Midnight Hunted

Mated by Midnight, book 2

By Heather Hildenbrand

Copyright © 2022. All rights reserved.

Edited by Dawn Y

Cover Design by Carol Marques Cover Design

MIDNIGHT FALLS, VIRGINIA

SUTTON'S HOUSE

2

SUTTON'S BOUNDARY LINE

STORE

TAILOR

BEAN THERE

MAIN STREET

LIBRARY

YVETTE'S B&B

1

SUTTON'S BOUNDARY LINE

MONIGHT FALLS

SUTTON'S BOUNDARY LINE

CHURCH

MAIN STREET

IFF'S OFFICE

YCAMORE STREET

oly shit. I'm trapped. The realization hits me the moment I open my eyes. It's the first thing on my mind just as it was the last thought I had before finally drifting off sometime before dawn. Not that those hours of sleep were particularly restful. Hard to find rest when my sleep is riddled with nightmares about how horribly I failed—and how there's no running away from any of this. Not anymore.

Groaning, I roll over and bury my face in the pillow. Sutton's scent hits me like a ton of bricks. No surprise, considering I spent the night in his bedroom—again. He'd offered to stay with me, but I'd refused—too upset about the party to want company. Okay, not so much the party as the murder and witchcraft and werewolves at the end.

Hell of a finale.

Most human parties end with fireworks, but, apparently, that's not enough for these people. Ugh. Not *people*. Not when every one of Midnight Falls' residents can once again shift at will into a wolf.

It was maybe the craziest moment of my life watching them all turn into four-legged predators at once. When the shock wore off, though, I recognized it for the opportunity it was. And I wasn't the only one.

With their wolf senses restored, the pack had tried hunting down Audrey and Yvette so we could end this, once and for all—due process be damned. But a full search of the town had yielded nothing. They'd simply … vanished. My only hope is that they're trapped just like I am. Hiding out somewhere nearby. Otherwise—I don't even want to consider what it means if they've managed to sneak out, leaving us trapped in here with nothing but a magical curse to contend with until next year's renewal.

One thing is certain, though: Nowhere is safe until they are found.

Gripping Sutton's pillow with one hand, I

breathe him in. Maybe having him here last night would have been a healthy distraction. A way to pass the time. I can't freak out about my nightmarish reality if I'm too busy orgasming...right?

Ugh. No.

It was my raging hormones that got me into this shitty predicament, and the last thing I need is to listen to them again. Who knows what'll happen if I slip again? Another murder? Refusing to let my hormones be the reason for another death, I force myself to get out of bed.

After crossing the room, I pause in front of the door. Shutting myself in here alone has cocooned me even just for a few hours. It let me pretend or try to forget the impossible reality of my life. When I leave this room, it all becomes horrifyingly real.

I'm trapped in Midnight Falls.

Being hunted by a woman—no, a witch—bent on revenge for a crime she, herself, committed.

And somehow, last night, I broke the part of her curse that was keeping the residents of this town trapped in their human forms. A flash of blue light and now they can shift at will again. Maybe that's good news for them, but for me, it only adds to the 'crazy.'

I double back to the mirror that hangs over the

sagging dresser. A hairline crack runs across the top edge of the reflective glass.

Seven years bad luck, I can't help but think.

Kind of sums up the turn my life has taken.

My gaze flicks to my reflection. Dark circles under my eyes. Rumpled hair. Deep lines around my mouth where I'm frowning without even realizing it.

I smooth my hair and school my features as best I can. Nothing is going to get solved with me hiding in this room. *Get your shit together, Serenity.*

With a deep breath, I step out into the hall and make my way down the stairs. The wooden floor-boards creak as I walk, the magic that restored the house to its prior beauty last night gone now that we're back to square one. And it *is* square one. With Sheriff Rhodes dead, his blood drained and gone, the curse has been renewed for another year.

I failed.

Honestly, the crumbling manor house is the least of my problems. But right now, it just adds to my pissed-off mood.

Muted male voices carry out of the kitchen, so I stop on the last step and listen.

"Things are different now." *Where have I heard that voice?*

"Maybe," Sutton replies. "But we're still no closer to breaking the curse." His voice wraps around me like an embrace, warming me from the inside. Guilt nags at me for pushing him away last night.

The familiar voice speaks again. "We are, though, don't you see? Serenity being here changes things."

Sutton doesn't immediately reply, so I wait, holding my breath for his response.

A response that comes in the form of him appearing around the corner and coming to a stop right in front of me. "Morning, beautiful."

His smile nearly knocks me on my ass, and I can't help but agree with the stranger. Some things *have* changed because Sutton Hargrave looks more relaxed than I've ever seen. And inner peace looks good as hell on this man's face. It's out of place amid such chaos but no less welcome. And it reminds me exactly where his face was last night in that library—before everything went to hell.

My heart flutters. "Morning. Am I interrupting?"

Another man comes around the corner from the kitchen, and I realize he's no stranger at all—at least, not entirely. "Good morning, Serenity," Phineas greets.

My eyes widen in surprise. As one of the few people to extend a friendly word to me in this town, Phineas is a more welcome sight than others. Still, I'm not sure what he's doing here, other than discussing me. And since neither man looks inclined to explain it, I let it go. For now. The journalist in me is all about strategic information gathering.

And I get the impression that badgering either of these men about anything will only result in more questions. "Morning. Coffee?" I ask, directing my attention to Sutton.

"Absolutely."

I step down, ignoring the way Sutton reaches for me. I know it's pathetic to try to pretend things are not as complex as they are between us, but honestly? I don't know how much more complicated I can take. Besides, he's the one keeping secrets and talking about me behind my back. Until I know why, I can't trust anyone. Not even Sutton. Letting my emotions cloud my judgment resulted in a man's death, and I won't repeat that mistake.

Phineas reaches for a paper cup still sitting in a

drink carrier then hands it to me. "Jolene said this is your favorite."

"Jolene?" I eye it warily.

"It's not poison," Sutton says as if the bastard can read my mind.

"Are you sure about that? She doesn't like me."

"You'll find things have changed since last night," Phineas says softly.

Sutton clears his throat and glares at Phineas.

"What's up your ass?" I demand. Then, deciding that if the coffee kills me, it wouldn't exactly be the worst thing at the moment, I take a drink. The hot liquid slips down the back of my throat, and I decide it *definitely* wouldn't be the worst way to go. The current threat to my life notwithstanding.

Phineas answers for him. "My son believes things are going to get worse before they get better."

Coffee spews out of my mouth and burns my nose. It splatters Sutton's once-white shirt, and I cough, barely managing to cling to my cup in the process.

Phineas reaches across the kitchen counter and retrieves a towel, offering it to me. I don't take it. Instead, I stand there, coffee all over my face, glaring at the two men, who are both trying to feign innocence.

"Excuse the shitballs out of me," I say, snatching the towel from my chess buddy's still outstretched hand. "Did you just say *son?* As in you're his—"

"I am Sutton's father," Phineas replies easily as though it's not a huge brick of knowledge he just dropped on my head.

"You're related." I look to Sutton, who shoves both hands into his pockets and quickly glances down at his feet.

"Yes," he says.

"And no one thought to give me this very interesting piece of information before?"

Sutton withdraws his hands and shrugs. "It wasn't pertinent."

"Are you fucking kidding me?" I roar, slamming the coffee down and dropping the towel so I can cross both arms. *"Not pertinent?* I had coffee with you," I gesture to Phineas. "Played chess. Told you about my family. Why didn't you tell me who you are to each other?"

His gaze darts to Sutton, telling me all I need to know. "I didn't think it was necessary, and I didn't want to put you in more danger."

Lie. I don't even bother addressing Phineas. Instead, I turn to Sutton. He's the one who had his tongue in my mouth last week and his face between my legs last night. Therefore, he's the one who *should* have been honest. It's not like there weren't plenty of opportunities for him to say, 'Hey, Serenity, say hi to my dear old dad for me, will you? His name is Phineas.'

"You told him not to tell me, didn't you?"

"That information wouldn't have helped."

"How the hell do you figure that?"

"Tell me how your knowledge of my familial relations would have assisted in discovering the identity of a witch?"

I glare at him. "It would have helped me trust you sooner."

"I didn't want to earn your trust by process of elimination," he replies sternly. "I wanted you to trust me because it's what you felt."

I shake my head, so pissed off I can barely formulate words. "You are both assholes," I announce then turn to Phineas. "You, less so."

He offers me a half-smile that tells me he understands, and I turn away, abandoning my coffee and marching back to the stairs.

As I climb, my eyes fill with tears as my throat

burns. Pushing into the room, I take a seat on the bed and rest my face in my hands. Tears flow freely down my cheeks as emotion burns my throat.

I came here wanting to solve these murders so no one else would die. And I failed. Miserably. The memory of Sheriff Rhodes lying in a pool of his own blood—what little was left of it anyway — surfaces.

Is this what Sutton feels like all the time? Useless and stuck?

The door creaks open, and I glare through angry tears at Sutton. He doesn't say anything, just crosses the room and takes a seat on the bed beside me. It dips with his weight, and I avert my gaze to the window.

"I should have told you," Sutton says calmly.

"Yeah, you should have. Any other family members you've left out?" I snap.

"Not living, no. My father is the only blood relative I have left."

The way he says it, the sad tone of his voice, *almost* makes me feel like an asshole for being pissed off. I look back at him. "I don't do secrets, Sutton. I get that you had them before you could trust me, but when it comes to this curse and the people involved, you'd damn well better be honest with me. I'm trapped here, too, which means this is also my fight. Do not keep me out of the loop again."

A muscle in his jaw ticks, but he nods.

I start to respond but am cut off when my ringtone fills the small room. "I thought I had no service —" I reach for it, more than surprised to see three bars and Steven's name illuminating the screen. Sniffling, I wipe a hand over my face before answering and do my best to clear the emotion from my voice. "Hello?"

"You're almost late."

I move an inch to the left, and the signal goes fuzzy. Jerking back again, I freeze in place where the call is clearest. "For what?"

"Calling me."

Shit. "I slept in. It was a long night."

"You have anything new for me?"

"No. I was wrong." The lie is bitter on my tongue. It tastes like deceit, and I fucking hate it. "Yvette is innocent, so we're back to square one over here."

"Serenity."

"Steven," I reply instantly. I know my brother. If I give him even the slightest hesitation, the smallest reservation, he will jump all over it. And the last thing I need is him bringing the National Guard into a town full of werewolves.

He sighs. "Why don't you just come home? It's not like you're relaxing anyway."

"Actually..." I pinch the bridge of my nose, hating myself for what I know I need to do. "I think I'm going to let the locals handle the case. I've started to enjoy hiking. And there are really beautiful waterfalls here."

More lies. My life seems to be built on them lately, something that makes me want to hurl myself off the nearest cliff. I'm no liar. Brutally honest? Sometimes. But I pride myself on always telling the truth.

"You're going to vacation in a town you traveled to in an attempt to investigate unsolved murders?"

"I'm perfectly safe."

"Then why do you sound like you've been crying?"

Damn. Steven's always been way too perceptive for his own freaking good. "Allergies, moron."

"Serenity," he warns.

I sigh. Might as well give him something good. "They gave my job away."

"What?"

"Allison called to let me know," I say. "Quincy is interviewing for my position at the paper."

It's not a lie that helps. It's also not exactly numero uno on my priority list, what with this magical curse and a witch trying to kill me. Still, letting my dream job slip through my fingers stings like a bitch.

"Damn, Ser. That sucks. I'm sorry."

"Yeah, so let's just say I'm running out of reasons to rush right back to the city."

"Look, I know it's hard, what you're going through, but this is a time for family. You need to come home." Clearly, I have not convinced him.

"No," I snap, a little ruder than I mean to be. "I'm not a little girl anymore, Steven, and I want to stay. This place is really great, and as far as I know, no new dead bodies have popped up."

I'm going to hell for that one, for sure.

Steven is silent for a few moments, something not unusual for him, but it still makes my skin crawl. I've never been good at tricking him, and if he senses anything is off— "Fine," he finally says. "But if anything happens, you need to come home, or I'll drive my ass out there to get you."

The very idea of him getting caught in this web makes my stomach roll. "I'll be fine, and I promise to check in. I'll send you lots of hiking pictures," I add.

"I love you, Ser. You're a massive pain in my ass, but life would suck without you. Don't tell the others, but if I had to pick, you'd be my favorite."

Tears spring to my eyes, and my chest tightens. "Love you, too, assface." I end the call and toss my cell to the bed before burying my face in both hands. Steven doesn't typically do feelings. He's straightforward, logical—so for him to be that soft on me… I choke on a sob. He's worried, and this time, he has every reason to be.

What if I never make it home?

"You lied to him."

"What the hell else was I supposed to say?" I whip my head toward Sutton, glaring through the tears. "I'm trapped in a town full of wolf people as I try to break a curse placed on the sexiest one of them, all by a witch who murdered her own daughter?" I snort and get to my feet, turning to face him. "Yeah, he would have taken to that really well."

Sutton grins at me and stands. He eats up the distance between us in two strides then reaches forward and cups my cheek. "I'm the sexiest one, huh?"

Rolling my eyes, I pull away. "That would be the only part you heard."

I start to head for the door, but he grips my arm and spins me back toward him. "My father is right. You gave me part of my life back. I'm not sure how, but you being here changes things, Serenity."

The pad of his thumb strokes my lip, and despite my guilt over lying to Steven, lust pools in my belly. Unable to help myself, I reach out and wrap my arms around Sutton, leaning into him and breathing deeply. "I'm trapped."

"We'll find a way to free you."

"There's no world in which I can stay here for a year without my family showing up, Sutton. And if they come here—"

"They will stay safe," he assures me.

I pull back and turn my face up to his. "They have to."

Sutton nods. The way he watches me, the smoldering heat in his gaze as it momentarily drops to my mouth and then back up, burns me.

But, just when I think he might lean in to kiss me, Sutton lets me go. "I need to go into town and meet with my pack."

Surprise spears through me, shoving past the

disappointment. "You can do that? But I thought you were confined here."

"I was. Until last night. Whatever you did... it opened the barrier between the woods and the town."

"That's how Phineas is able to be here right now," I realized. How the hell did I miss that little nugget of information? Oh, yeah, Daddy Phineas.

He nodded. "It's been a very long time since I've stepped foot in that town. I honestly cannot wait." Hope shines brightly on his handsome face. "We're going to organize patrols and search parties so we can look for Audrey and Yvette. Do you want to come?"

The excitement in his eyes is unmistakable. He doesn't just have to go. He wants to. But I can't. Not if it means facing everyone. Guilt crushes down on me, eliminating the rest of whatever lust his touch stirred. "No."

"Ser—"

"I am the reason the Sheriff is dead," I tell him. "And they already hated me before."

He shakes his head and reaches forward to take my hands. The pads of his thumbs run along the tops, but I can barely feel it, far too focused on the realization that, not only am I trapped, but I'm stuck in a town where the majority of the population despises me. "They don't hate you. Especially not now," he insists.

Even if that's true, fear and defeat keep me rooted. Besides, what the hell would I wear? My clothes are all still in the B&B, and the dress I wore last night is a no-go, mainly because I plan to burn it at the first convenient moment. Nothing Audrey made will touch my body again. I highly doubt they would take kindly to me showing up in Sutton's shorts and baggy t-shirt.

Nothing. "I don't want to go, Sutton."

His expression falters, disappointment passing over his handsome features, but he nods and releases my hands. "I'll be back as soon as I can."

I don't answer.

He turns to leave, and I take a deep breath before plopping back onto the mattress. Minutes pass as I stare at the ceiling above me, contemplating all the positives.

One: things could be worse than being trapped with Sutton.

Two: nope. There's pretty much just the one.

This town never felt suffocating before, but right now, knowing I can't leave, that there's no way out—it's more confining than I've ever felt. So, getting to my feet, I head back downstairs to retrieve my abandoned coffee so I can get started making a list of everything I know.

Research. Logic. Working through the facts. It's what I do best. And with Sutton's library catalog, I should be able to come up with something I didn't know before. Some piece to this curse-riddled puzzle that's now mine to solve whether I want it or not.

I'm just rounding the corner into the kitchen when I realize I'm not alone.

Phineas smiles at me and gestures to a chess board he's set out on the dinette. He looks nervous, almost, uncomfortable, and it makes me feel a little guilty for my earlier outburst even as warranted as it was.

"Care to join me?" he asks.

"I—"

"I'm very sorry for my deceit," he says quickly, interrupting me.

"No apology necessary," I reply, my anger toward him deflating like a week-old balloon. "He's your son. I get it." Grabbing my coffee, I take a seat at the table, and he sits across from me. "I wish he would have told me, though."

"Sutton is..." Phineas trails off as he moves his pawn forward. "Complicated."

"Understatement."

He chuckles, but the amusement fades quickly, a shadow passing over his usually open expression. "Myrtle—the witch who cursed us—hated my family for what happened to her daughter. She killed Vivian first, knowing how much it would hurt. And it does, of course, but out of all three of us, Sutton was punished the greatest. Being trapped out here, surrounded by memories—" The man's eyes mist, and I know he's recalling his late wife.

Reaching over, I cover his hand with mine. "Sutton told me what happened to her. I'm so sorry."

Swallowing hard, he nods. "She was my life. My everything. Losing Sutton on top of it, even in the way I did, it nearly killed me."

"I can't even imagine."

Phineas pulls his hand from beneath mine and swipes his fingertips under both eyes. "Knowing he was out here and not being able to touch him, to talk to him—" He shakes his head angrily. "I have carried so much rage and grief all these years. And knowing Yvette and Audrey were right under my nose—"

"You couldn't have known," I assure him. "No one did."

He takes a deep breath and nods. "You did. You suspected Yvette."

"Outsiders perspective," I tell him. "Easier to see when you don't have any kind of attachment."

"Maybe." He reaches across and takes one of my hands, his gaze meeting mine. "You gave me my son back, Serenity. I am forever in your debt."

"Help me figure out how to get the hell out of here, and we'll call it even."

Chapter Two

P hineas and I spend two hours scouring the downstairs library for any books that might offer a clue about the details of this curse and how to break it. I start with the books Sutton stole out from under me when I first began researching. The thief, I now know, was Phineas himself. They'd wanted to ensure I came to Sutton for help rather than going up against Audrey on my own. But in the end, there's nothing useful inside their pages, making his theft by proxy a moot effort.

Empty-handed, we return to the kitchen where Phineas proceeds to kick my ass at chess, not once but twice. I go with it, mostly because I need a bit of normalcy after the crazy twenty-four hours I've had, not to mention the complete dead-end we just hit in the library. Something about the black and white rules of chess are a comfort amidst the real-life chaos going on now.

By the time Phineas has set up the board for a third game, my stomach is growling with a serious and sudden need for food. Phineas lifts a brow, letting me know he heard it too.

"Sounds like someone missed breakfast," he says.

I'm surprised then delighted as Phineas jumps up and begins making sandwiches for us both. He moves about the kitchen, clearly comfortable. And why wouldn't he be? Before Audrey ruined his life, this *was* his home.

"How does it feel?" I ask cautiously. "Being back here after everything?"

Phineas sighs and continues spreading mayonnaise on a piece of white bread. "It feels natural," he replies. "And a bit empty. My Vivian brought sunshine into every room she walked into. Sutton is a bit like her in that sense, I suppose."

I snort, and he grins at me, arching a dark eyebrow. "You don't agree?"

"He's been quite broody since we met."

Chuckling, Phineas reaches into the refrigerator and pulls out some cheese. "I imagine being trapped here alone has changed him. My hope is that you will help bring that side of him back."

He says it so easily, so casually, it catches me off guard. "How will I bring it back?"

After adding some sliced turkey to the top of the cheese, he squeezes a bit of mustard on top and closes the sandwich. Then, he slides it across the counter to me. "I'm no fool," he says. "I can see the way the two of you look at each other. A look I recognize because I had the very same one with my wife."

My stomach twists, a vice closing around my heart at the same time. "Sutton and I are— Things are complicated."

He finishes prepping the second sandwich then puts everything in the fridge and moves around to join me. "Sutton has this selfless side that I can't help but admire. It's why he makes a much better leader than I ever was. But I always wondered if one day he'd meet the woman who would make him yearn to be a bit selfish."

"And you think that woman is me?" Not one to beat around the bush, I don't see the point in pretending we're talking about someone else.

"I do," he says easily before taking a bite of his sandwich. "Though I imagine you're considering all the ways I'm wrong," he adds as soon as he swallows.

"There are quite a few."

He shrugs and grins. "Then I suppose only time will tell."

I take a bite of my sandwich and nearly groan in response to the food. Shit, I don't even know when the last time I ate was. I guess at the library yesterday? "This is delicious, thank you."

"Anytime."

"Are wolves usually this nurturing?" I ask after another bite.

"Excuse me?"

"Sutton cooks for me, always has fresh coffee brewed, and now you're making me lunch."

"Ah." He relaxes and wipes his hands on his napkin. "My wife taught us both how to cook and care for our own needs—beat us over the head with it, actually."

I suppress a smile. "Hopefully not literally."

"If that's what it took."

"She sounds like a very fascinating woman."

"My Vivian was one of a kind," he says wistfully and takes a drink of water.

"I wish I could have met her."

"She would have loved you."

For several minutes, we eat in silence, and I'm struck by how easy the quiet is between us. Phineas isn't a replacement for my own father, but he's definitely the next best thing. A source of comfort in the middle of a terrifying situation.

"Can I ask you a question?"

Phineas sits back, his expression genuine. "Anything."

"That blue spark last night," I say and watch as his open expression immediately shuts down again, but I press on. "The one that flashed just before everyone became wolves... that came from me, didn't it?"

"What do you think?" he asks, and I scowl.

"I asked you first."

His lips twitch. "Fair enough." Then he rubs at the stubble along his chin. "Yes, I think it's safe to say that blue spark came from you."

His honesty has me leaning forward in earnest. "How?"

He shakes his head. "That's not something I can answer."

My eyes narrow. "What about Sutton?" I ask. "Can he answer it?"

Phineas tries to bite back a smile. "My son has his own ideas about you and what he thinks is best."

"Keeping secrets, you mean. And lies."

His brow lifts. "He doesn't lie, and neither do I." When I open my mouth to argue, he adds, "We leave out details at times, but we won't lie. Not to you, Serenity. I swear it."

I want to believe him. But the last twenty-four hours have left me reeling. And that blue spark feels important. Like there's something about me I don't know. Add that to their private pow-wow this morning, and the questions are piling up way faster than the answers.

"At the party, Audrey said she'd been waiting for me."

"Did she now?"

He rubs at his beard again, and I swallow back the impatience that rises. My need for answers is overwhelming. Almost as consuming as the guilt of my failure.

I want to ask him the real question: about what I am and what I did last night to help free the wolves from whatever Audrey had done to bind them. But then I remember the blue flame Audrey conjured... How familiar it felt. How drawn to its power I was. And I'm suddenly afraid of what Phineas might tell me. Maybe there's a reason for his half-answers. I've always sought the truth—no matter how twisted or painful it might be. But maybe, just maybe, this time I should wait. Because I can't help but wonder if the answer won't reveal me to be less of the hero and more of the villain.

After all, magic is what cast this curse in the first place.

"I take it the sandwich was terrible," he quips, giving me a change of subject I didn't realize I needed.

I look down at my empty plate and snort. "Oh, yeah. Terrible."

He chuckles, and I release a heavy breath—and my frustration with it. Phineas is not the enemy here. In fact, he's been nothing but kind to me.

"You know, being fed by two caring, handsome men could make a girl forget she can't leave town," I tease.

"That's the idea." Phineas winks.

I laugh, surprised to find I can still find any humor in it all. But then a figure moves in the doorway, and my smile vanishes.

Sutton's gaze collides with mine, and there's a shift in the air that I feel straight to my core. His presence fills the space more than his physical form ever could, but it's more than that. It's his mood. He looks way too serious for the lighthearted moment

Phineas and I were having. And the way he's watching me? The hardened gaze trained directly on me? It's way too damn hot for my liking.

He shares a look with Phineas that honestly makes me wonder if they can communicate telepathically. To prove my point, Phineas rises from his seat. He sets his empty plate beside the sink and says, "Well, that's my cue." He looks at me. "I'll be back in the morning, and we'll see if we have better luck, deal?"

"Deal," I tell him.

He squeezes my shoulder on his way out.

Sutton doesn't say a word. Even when we're alone, the silence stretches, and without Phineas as a buffer, it feels awkward. Or maybe I'm afraid I'm going to respond to whatever subliminal message he's trying to send me and strip naked right here to finish what we started in that library of his last night.

It's tempting.

And that's exactly why I can't let myself do it.

"How'd it go with the pack?" I ask, feeling strange about using that word.

But he nods and crosses to the sink where he fills a glass full of water. "Good. The teams are set up, and we have a schedule worked out so no one's on shift alone. Hopefully, something will turn up soon."

By "something" he means Audrey. Or Yvette. Preferably both.

My stomach clenches at the image of their faces burned into my memory. The idea of facing them again both boils my blood and terrifies me, all at the same time. Two contrasting forces, both with the power to send me into a full-on spiral.

Sutton lifts the water glass and empties the contents in one long swig. When he lowers it again, his gaze is steady and trained on me. I recognize the look he wears now. It's the same one he gave me in that library last night just before he buried his face between my legs. My insides curl in anticipation at the same time my heart shutters closed against the prospect of letting him get that close to me again.

"Well, I should get started on that research," I say, pushing to my feet and heading for the door.

Sutton rounds the counter and plants his feet, blocking my escape. "Serenity." My name is rough in his throat, and it sends a shiver down my spine. "We should talk."

"Sutton," I begin, ready to shut him down, but he doesn't give me a chance to finish.

He takes a step forward, and I retreat, repeating

the actions until I am trapped between his hard body and the wall. Slowly, as if I'm breakable, he lifts his hand to my cheek and trails his fingertips gently down my face. Hunger reflects back at me from the depths of his eyes. I blink away a sudden rush of hot tears, desperate to give him what he wants. Most of me wants it too.

"Last night, we—"

"Last night we were stupid," I snap before he can say something dirty or romantic. Either one will completely shatter my control.

His brows knit in confusion. "How can you say that?"

"C'mon, Sutton. You know it's true. If we hadn't been so distracted, we might have actually found a way to stop Audrey before she killed Rhodes. We might even have broken the curse completely. Instead, I let myself forget my real reason for being here, and now someone is dead because of my carelessness."

"This isn't your fault," he says quietly.

"Isn't it?" I shoot back. "What was that blue spark last night, Sutton? I know you saw it, and we both know it came from me. Whatever it was, it gave everyone their ability to shift again, didn't it?"

He grimaces. "We don't have to talk about this right now."

"No? But we can have sex, right? We can sleep together, but telling me the truth is where you draw the line." He doesn't respond, though the harshness in his gaze tells me I'm getting to him. *Good.* "What are you hiding from me?" I demand.

Pulling back, he crosses his arms. "I'm not hiding anything."

"Bull shit. Did I do magic? Am I a witch like Audrey? Tell me the truth. No more secrets, remember?"

His sigh holds the weight of the world in it. "Yes, it was magic. And yes, it gave everyone their shifting ability back."

"How?" I ask in a small voice.

"I don't know," he admits. "I spent all day trying to find out. I wanted answers before I came to you."

"And did you find any?"

"Not yet."

"You shouldn't have kept it from me. Especially after our conversation."

"I wanted answers, Serenity. Answers that, for once, wouldn't lead to more questions since we both have enough of those."

He's right, but that doesn't mean I can give myself over to my feelings. In fact, it only strengthens my decision not to. "Well, I intend to figure all of this out. And that's exactly why I can't take things any further with you. Not while the curse has us both trapped."

He cocks his head, studying me intently. "You think I want to be with you because we're trapped together?"

"No, of course not." I say the words with much more confidence than I feel. "Look, you've lived this reality for a century. And, well, it's probably been a while, hasn't it?"

I expect him to get angry. Defensive. Instead, he arches an eyebrow and cocks his head to the side. "So you believe I want to sleep with you because—what—it's been a while and you're the closest opportunity?"

Swallowing hard, I stand my ground even when he takes a step closer. "You will never be a convenience for me," he replies. "And I've done just fine on my own the past century. Believe it or not, I want more than sex from you."

Even as I fight it, the image of Sutton pleasuring himself slams into me. I blink rapidly, trying to shut it out, but not before it pushes my own libido into overdrive.

"Fine. Good for you. You know how to play with yourself. But, as I said before you de-railed us, you've known this reality for a long time. I've known it for less than a day. I just... I can't think about my own feelings when lives are on the line. Not after last night."

"First of all, Serenity, I don't 'play'. In *anything* I do. Second, I've already told you that this isn't your fault."

"You're their alpha," I say, completely ignoring yet another wave of heat. "You can't tell me you don't feel responsible for what happens to the people in this town."

Something flashes in his eyes. Anger, maybe. But he doesn't contradict me.

"What I feel for you is more than a mere distraction," he replies, his voice cracking with emotion.

My heart aches because, two days ago, I would have given my right tit to hear him say that to me. But now, it only strengthens my resolve. "That's exactly my point," I say, heartbreak softening my words. "These people are counting on me. On us. If someone else dies because I lost focus—again—I wouldn't be able to live with myself."

I can barely live with myself now.

I don't say that part out loud, but I know he sees it in my eyes because he takes a step back. It's a small step, but it's a retreat nonetheless. And I know it means he's giving up. For some reason, that makes me want to cry.

"I have to find a way to free them," I add softly. "And you." *And me.* "Until I do that, I can't let myself feel things for you."

"You can't stop feeling," he says. "It doesn't work that way."

I shake my head, willing him to be wrong even though I know he isn't. "It has to."

Chapter Three

J ust outside the bedroom window, the sun crests over the mountains. I've already been awake for hours, though. Mostly texting with Allison, which can only be done if I sit in a very specific position with one leg higher than the other and my phone tilted to the left. It's ridiculous, but I needed girl talk too badly not to deal with the horrible signal I get out here. After our confrontation yesterday, Sutton left, and I haven't seen him since. I can feel him though, his presence, yet another oddity I cannot explain.

One more damned question that lacks an answer.

But it's how I know he was merely avoiding me and hadn't actually left.

It's also how I know he's already gone this morning. The warmth I feel when he's near, the tingling of awareness, is no longer there. In its place is an absence that feels oddly lonely.

Still, it's another day. A chance to find out how to break this damned curse so I can leave this town and forget all about it and its ridiculously sexy, broody leader. Or take him to bed with me. I can't let myself choose either until the curse is done.

Judging by her last text, Allison is clearly on Team Sutton, which doesn't help matters.

Whoever this "S" mystery man is—I'm calling it: S stands for SEX, girl! Get you some!

I didn't tell her about the magical curse or town full of werewolves, obviously. Only that I'm trying to resist feelings for a guy because I don't want to let him be nothing more than a convenient rebound from Roscoe. She doesn't seem to follow my logic.

Tossing my phone aside, I force my ass up and out of bed for another riveting day in Midnight Falls. Dressed in a pair of baggy shorts and a sweatshirt I pilfered from Sutton's closet, I pull open the bedroom door and step out into the hall —only to nearly trip over something blocking my exit. With a hand on the wall, I barely manage to keep my feet under me. The culprit, a black duffel, sits on the floor with a note boasting my name.

Curious, I reach down and lift both then head back into the bedroom and set the bag on the bed before opening the note.

Serenity,

I thought this might help with your lack of supplies. I'll be out most of the day but will be back at four to get you for the funeral.

-S

Funeral. My stomach rolls, and I toss the note to the side. As much as I want to skip it, I know I can't. Regardless of how shitty I feel, not paying respects to the man who tried to warn me would be far worse. Sheriff Rhodes deserves at least that.

Swallowing hard, I unzip the bag and nearly weep with joy when I see an assortment of women's clothing and toiletries inside. All of my emotional turmoil momentarily pushed aside, I reach in and start pulling the items out.

Lavender scented body wash, actual shampoo— my hormones lean hard toward Allison's way of thinking as I picture Sutton picking all this out for me. I waste no time stripping out of Sutton's clothes and redressing in a pair of black leggings and an oversized baby blue sweatshirt before stashing the shampoo, conditioner, and soap in Sutton's shower for later.

All dressed up with nowhere to go, I head downstairs and smile at Phineas as he pours a steaming mug of coffee. But then my gaze shifts to the pile of groceries on the island and the gift baskets sitting beside it.

"Go shopping?" I ask.

He chuckles and offers me a mug. "Hardly. Those are gifts. For you."

I narrow my gaze at him then turn back toward the stack. "What do you mean for me?"

"The town is very grateful for what you've done. This is how they show it. Be glad it's not dead animals."

I blanch, my stomach churning. "Why the hell would it be—" And then it dawns on me. "You're wolves."

He smiles widely. "Wolves who have been unable to access half of ourselves for a hundred years. We owe you a lot, Serenity."

"I don't want gifts. I sure as hell don't deserve them. It's my fault someone is dead."

His gaze darkens. "It's not your fault. The blame lies solely with the witch."

"I—" My explanation dies on my lips. How do

you tell a man you let a murder happen because you were too busy letting his son devour you like you were the last macaroon in the box? "I was distracted the night she killed him. If I'd been focused—"

"Then you might have been the one killed." He reaches over and gently touches my shoulder. "Do not underestimate what you granted us. Let them be grateful. Not accepting the gifts will offend them."

Unease swirls in my belly. I've never been good at receiving gifts—but this? This is way too damned much. And it's completely undeserved. The mistakes I've made since coming here have been many, and ignoring that won't change it.

I thought I'd been brave. Determined. But really, I'd been stupid. How the hell could I have thought I had what it would take to solve these murders? To stop them? Granted, I'd had no idea just what I was getting into. At least, not until Sutton had warned me.

He'd begged me to leave, to get myself out and come back when it was safe, and I'd ignored him. Arrogance, determination, stubbornness, whatever you want to call it, the fact still remains that this curse is more than any human can handle. Magic is not something to trifle with. And I did it anyway.

Now, I'm paying the price.

We all are.

If I had just listened, I could have come back the next morning and not been trapped. And maybe if I could leave, I could head back to New York and try to pull some strings to bring in real help. The idea of trying to explain any of this to Steven tells me that's not exactly a solid plan, either.

"Get out of your head, girl," Phineas says softly. "Regrets will get you nowhere."

"I wish I could," I reply. "Thanks for the coffee."

He smiles softly. "Anytime. What can I do to help today?"

"We need to finish going through the books in Sutton's library—or I guess it's yours."

Shaking his head, he beams at me. "That is Sutton's. This house, all of it. I'm merely here for you."

"Thank you," I say again, my heart warming. "I really appreciate it."

"No need to thank me." He claps his hands together. "Let's go get some reading done."

"This is useless." Groaning, I toss the book down onto Sutton's desk and run both hands over my face.

"It has definitely been a fruitless venture, hasn't it?"

I glance up at Phineas, who is pacing the room with a leather-bound book in his hand. Between the tweed vest and his glasses, he looks incredibly studious, and it makes me smile. He and my dad would totally get along. Not to mention the original hand-drawn map of the Falls I found and the amount of history in these volumes we've uncovered. Dad would be a kid in a candy store right about now.

And that thought brings a wave of pain down onto me. My parents are going to be heartbroken if I can't get out of here. If I miss a year's worth of dinners... Hell, they'll probably come here—I jump up from the chair, panic racing through my veins.

"We have got to figure this out."

Phineas turns toward me. "Are you all right?"

"No. Yes. I don't freaking know. But I just realized that if I don't solve this, I'm likely going to have all of the Kellis family members descending on this town to try to drag me out. And then—what if she finds them? What if she hurts them to get to me?"

All the horrific worse-case scenarios begin to pile on top of one another. Yvette knows my name. They know where I lived before here. They could easily track my family down. And since they're damned witches—

"They will not harm your family, Serenity."

I look up into Phineas' kind eyes. He's abandoned the book and managed to move directly in front of me without me even knowing. "You don't know my family."

"Yvette and Audrey didn't harm you, right? Both had ample opportunity, yet neither made a move. Their issue is not with you or your family."

I know he's placating me, trying to ease my anxiety, but it's not going to work. Not when we just discussed his late wife—and what Audrey did to her all those years ago. I'd known coming to investigate homicides could potentially put me in harm's way, but I never, not for a second, considered the effect it could have on my loved ones.

"I need to go call my mom."

"You can't tell her about this place."

"Don't you think I know that?" The words come out harsher than I meant, but Phineas' calm expression doesn't change. "I haven't had a chance to really talk to her since I came here. I need to go call her."

"I'll keep looking." He nods at the door, encouraging me to go.

I turn and head for the stairs, fighting tears the entire way up to my room. As soon as I'm safely inside, I take a deep, steadying breath, and wipe my face with the sleeve of my sweatshirt.

Then, I reach for my phone, praying my signal is strong enough to make this call, and tap Mom's contact information.

Holding the phone out, I wait for her to answer. Finally, after two rings, her flushed face comes into view on the screen. "Serenity," she greets, a broad smile on her face. "How are you, honey?"

"Hey, Mom." I smile at her, and if she notices it's not real, she doesn't comment. "I'm doing good. Just got up a little bit ago."

"Is that Serenity?" I hear Dad ask in the background, and my chest tightens.

"It is. Come say hi." Mom waves him over.

Dad's face pops into view, and he smiles, the lines at the corners of his eyes deepening. "Hey there, sweetie. How is that little town?"

"It's good," I lie. "Relaxing." Double lie.

"If you're sleeping in, you must be truly relaxing," Mom comments. "Good for you."

"I am getting plenty of sleep. I even learned a bit of chess so I can give Dad a run for his money when I get home."

Dad beams at me so warmly, and the ice in my veins thaws just enough that I can offer a genuine smile back. "I can't wait to see."

"How in the world did you learn chess all the way down there?" Mom asks.

"They have a really neat town center here," I tell them. "I met a guy who talked me into a game."

"Oh, really?" Mom grins and glances at Dad.

"Not that kind of guy." I snort.

"Have you met that kind of guy?" Mom questions, and my dad pales.

"Not here for this conversation. Love you, Ser, see you soon?"

"Maybe. I think I'm going to extend my time here a bit longer. I really love it here."

"We miss you at family dinners," my mom says softly. "Though, I am so proud you're taking a break. I imagine after the whole Roscoe thing—"

"I really do not want to talk about Roscoe," I interrupt.

Mom smiles. "Understood. How is everything

else? You eating okay?"

"I am. Everything is fine, promise."

"Good." She glances off-screen then looks back. "I need to get to my spin class. Can you call me later? I've missed our chats, but I didn't want to bother you."

"You're never a bother," I say quickly. "I'll give you a call when I get a chance. I love you Mom, love you, Dad."

"We love you, too, sweet pea. Talk soon."

The call ends, and I stare at my phone screen as a tear slips free from my eye. My heart aches with emptiness. I never realized just how much I counted on the routine of family dinners until I was unable to attend. Isn't that the bittersweet truth of it all, though?

You never realize what you have until it's gone.

Life is short. Sometimes way too short. And now, who the hell knows when I'll get to see my family again? When I'll get to hug my mother or see my nieces and nephews?

I toss the phone to the side and take a deep breath.

"Are you all right?"

Sutton's voice slams into me, and in my emotional state, I very nearly rush over to where he stands across the room and throw myself into his arms. Instead, I sit up, swiping at the tears staining my cheeks.

With a cup of coffee clutched in his hand, Sutton remains in the doorway, watching me. My gaze drifts to the dark suit he's wearing, much like the one I first saw him in. His jaw is freshly shaven, his eyes boring into me as though they can see straight through to my soul. I could tell him the truth. That I feel broken, lost, aimless, hopeless— but I know that if I let my walls down with Sutton now, I'll never leave him. Hell, I might even stop caring that I'm trapped at all. Somehow, that feels worse than fighting and losing. Giving up is not something I'm programmed for.

Despite my sadness, my heart flutters at the way he watches me. He doesn't make a move toward me, doesn't say another word. And I honestly can't tell if he's treating me like I'm fragile for my sake or his. But I hate it. Just once, I long to be reckless, stupid. And damn, I wish the weight of this little slice of the world wasn't resting on our shoulders.

"Fine. I just miss my family."

Sutton nods, but he doesn't press me for more. I know my rejection has hurt him, but I can't take it back.

"I wanted to let you know it's nearly time." He reaches behind him and retrieves a garment bag he must have draped on the balustrade when he'd walked up.

"Is that for me?"

"A gift. From Cara. She knew you didn't have anything besides—"

He doesn't finish.

We both know he means the dress I wore to the ball. And we both also know I'll never wear that thing again.

Silent, he crosses the room and sets the mug on the nightstand beside me. Then, he lays the bag down on the bed, though he doesn't move away. We're inches from one another, so close I can all but feel the body heat radiating from him.

"You're killing me," he growls.

"How?" I tilt my face up to look at him and lose my breath. Sutton closes his eyes and breathes deeply, the action sending my heart racing within my chest.

"I can sense your feelings," he whispers. "Even if you want to deny them. And knowing that you're just as aroused as I am, that you want me as badly as I want you, yet I cannot act on it, it's driving me mad."

"I..." Words fail me. Because I have no good argument other than we cannot allow ourselves to be distracted—something that I know Sutton does not agree with. So, I swallow hard and try to do what Allison said she's done in the past—I think about softball.

That does the trick, at least enough to break whatever hold we both had on each other—for now.

Sutton takes a step away from me. Then another. "I'll be downstairs. We need to leave in thirty minutes to make it in time."

Swallowing hard, I nod but continue to stare at the bag as he leaves. As soon as the door is shut softly behind him, I reach out and unzip the bag. The dress is simple. A black "V" neck with heavy lace that hits just below my knee. Simple—but elegant. Cara somehow nailed my style, and I make a mental note to thank her for the gesture.

I've only ever been to one funeral in my life. When my grandmother passed away, I was only ten, but I can recall every moment of that day. From my mother's swollen eyes as she helped my grief-stricken father to the car, to the pleats of my black dress and the casket's reflection in my shiny black shoes.

It had been sad and awkward all at the same

time because I hadn't known how to act. Steven was there, though, holding my hand and telling me that it was okay to cry.

I'd barely known the woman, and still, I'd wept for her.

And I hadn't caused her death. Not like I caused the Sheriff's.

There's no Steven here. No one to hold my hand. And certainly no one to help me face the crowd of people who—despite the gifts they've sent over—likely blame me for his death.

Still, I've never been a coward. So, with a deep breath, I dress, slipping into the black fabric and throwing my hair in a low ponytail. I reach into the bag and withdraw a pair of black flats from the bottom along with a small, hand-written note.

Hope these fit. I had to guess your size.

-Cara

I put them on, pleased to find they're a perfect fit, then head down the stairs.

Phineas is gone, leaving Sutton standing at the front door like we're headed to some twisted, dark prom night. The daydream is so far from reality it makes me want to scream, but it's in my mind before I can filter it out. Hands sweaty, I rub them on the black lace of the skirt, but it itches my skin.

"I'm ready," I say, and Sutton nods.

"I know I shouldn't say it, but you look beautiful."

"Beautiful for a funeral," I deadpan.

As I'm passing by, Sutton gently grips my arm, stopping me in place. "What happened to him was not your fault, Serenity. You can either keep beating yourself up or move forward, but you can't do both." He releases me and steps aside as I move toward the door.

I don't make it far, though, because I nearly trip over a bouquet of crimson roses someone has left on the top step. Sutton's quick maneuvering helps to keep me from trampling the flowers. He bends down and lifts them up, offering them to me.

"What the hell are these for?" I snap, a hell of a lot ruder than I meant.

He presses them into my arms. "For you."

"You got me flowers?"

Anger flits through me, setting my temper ablaze. I told him what I expected from him—friendship, nothing more. And today is absolutely not the day for romance, no matter what either of us wants. Especially when I can't help but notice how the red roses remind me of blood against our black clothes.

He shakes his head. "Not me."

"Then who...?"

I wait as he bends down again and picks up a small silver box. It's dainty with an intricately carved design covering all four sides. He offers it to me, taking the flowers so I can hold the box.

I stare down at it, not sure how to feel about the fact that my name has been carved into the lid. Opening it carefully, I withdraw a small folded note.

Fate has favored us at last. Destiny is on your side, and so are we.

It isn't signed, but the words themselves make my gut churn. I want to send it back. The note, the box, the flowers, the gifts from earlier. The sentiment. It's all wrong. All of this is wrong.

"Who did this?" I ask, my stomach roiling. Hands shaking, I all but fling the box and note at Sutton.

He studies the writing, then meets my gaze. "I don't know."

I narrow my eyes. "This is your place. You mean you didn't notice someone right outside? I thought your wolf senses—"

"There have been many people," he tells me.

"What do you mean?"

"You've had several visitors these last few days."

"What visitors?"

"Cara. She brought your dress. Jolene with the coffee. Then there was Mable. She brought dinner and a few other gifts from the others."

The gifts from earlier. The baskets from town. But if I'd known it was Cara and Mable— "Why didn't you tell me?"

He sighs. "Because I didn't want to alarm you or make you uncomfortable. My father told me you weren't overly thrilled by the gifts earlier, but"—he gestures to the box—"they want you to know they support you."

My heart sinks. The presents, the visitors—it's all to woo me. So I'll give them what they want. So I'll break their curse. Except I don't know how, and even if I did, I'm not sure why they think I'm strong enough when they clearly aren't.

I turn away.

"We should go. I don't want to be late." My tone is emotionless, but I can't be bothered to care. Mainly because I care too fucking much. Especially about the man I want nothing more than to lean into when I feel so broken inside.

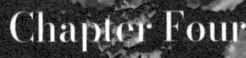

Chapter Four

The funeral is being held at Midnight Falls Chapel, a quaint little building that sits on the edge of town. I can still recall my initial impression of the small church I'd passed when I first arrived in Midnight Falls. Shit, my arrival that day feels like it happened a lifetime ago now. That version of me would have never imagined I'd be attending the funeral of the town Sheriff. Yet, here I am, walking inside a building that I'd initially thought was a tad on the creepy side to honor a man who wasn't even my friend to begin with.

Today, the small building is packed with people. And unlike the day I arrived and walked the streets of downtown, they don't whisper and stare at the sight of me. Instead, when they see us coming, the crowd parts in reverent silence, giving us clear passage straight to the front.

Sutton doesn't seem to expect anything less. Our progress slows as he pauses to greet people. It's clear he knows every one of them by name. It's impressive and endearing, the affection and respect they offer him. The obvious relief—joy, even—at being reunited.

For the first time since the party, I allow myself to focus on what this town gained instead of what I lost that night. And I'm glad to have played a part in Sutton's freedom, such as it is.

Still, after two days shut inside Sutton's library, I'm no closer to understanding how Audrey has trapped me here. Or what I did to break the parts of the curse that let these people shift into their wolves again. I've been thrust into a new world, one I don't understand, and by an enemy I am not nearly strong enough or smart enough to contend with.

Arden's lifeless body is proof of that. He's been lain out in a dark walnut casket that's surrounded by piles of flower arrangements. The casket lid is open, offering mourners one last goodbye. From here, I can see the dark fabric of his suit contrasting starkly with his pasty skin. His body has been cared for and cleaned, but the powdery coating of makeup across his cheeks makes me cringe.

I can't bring myself to move any closer.

When Sutton leads me to a seat in the front row and gestures for me to sit, I hesitate, not sure I have a right to this space reserved for close friends and family. Then again, from the looks of it, Arden Rhodes had no family. The bench is nearly empty save for one face I recognize.

"Serenity." Mable, the town librarian, reaches over and takes my hand, gently pulling me down beside her on the bench. "How are you, dear?" she asks quietly. "Holding up all right?"

"I'm fine," I tell her as my insides tense with the lie.

"Did you get the fruit basket I sent over?"

"I did, yes. Thank you."

I feel suddenly guilty for resisting the gifts. Mable is sweet. She's never been anything but nice to me—even when others weren't. Still, it's hard to imagine little old Mable shifting into a deadly wolf. The image is a bit amusing, in fact. Granny as the Big Bad Wolf.

"You need anything else, you let me know, all right? The library is yours to use as you see fit. Oh, here." She presses a tissue into my hand. "Just in case."

I take the tissue and ball it up in my fist. My heart warms at Mable's kindness then squeezes as Phineas steps up to the podium. He clears his throat and looks out over the quieting room.

"Thank you all for coming."

Sutton sits down on my other side. The heat of his body is an awareness I can't ignore even at a somber event like this. We're magnets, him and I. Forever drawn to each other, no matter how many reasons we have to stay away. Reasons that are becoming more irrelevant by the minute if my hormones have any say in the matter.

Once, I held back because I thought he was a monster. Now, I hold back because I am. "We're gathered here today to honor the life of Sheriff Arden Rhodes," Phineas says, and my eyes blur with hot tears, my focus returning to the casket up front and the man inside it, put there by my failure. "Arden was a friend to many of us, but he was also a protector. He dedicated his life to law enforcement and service to the people. He made sacrifices for that role. And in the end, he made the ultimate sacrifice for every one of us who call this town home."

Phineas pauses to collect himself, and it's all I can do to stay where I am. My hands fist tightly with the urge to run from this room. To scream. To beat on something—or someone. Anything to make sense of what happened. But there's nothing sensible about murder.

As Phineas talks about the life of a man I barely knew, I take deep, measured breaths to keep from falling apart. The rest of the room is silent other than a few sniffles and coughs. Mable dabs her eyes with a crinkly tissue. Beside me, Sutton is rigidly stoic. Once, his hand twitches, and I wonder if he's about to reach for me. But he doesn't, and I don't know whether I'm disappointed or relieved.

At the podium, Phineas offers a final prayer, and then it's over. My gaze locks on the casket as two men move forward and close the lid, securing the recently departed inside.

It feels smothering even watching.

I swallow hard as six more men join the two—then again as they take their places on both sides of the casket. They reach down and lift, and I stand with the crowd as the Sheriff's body is carried down the aisle and out the door.

"Thank you all for coming." Sutton's voice pulls me back, and I realize he's moved up onto the stage.

I quickly sit down, not wanting to feel like an intruder on this moment.

"If any of you need anything, please feel free to come find me. My door is always open to the pack." His gaze drifts to mine briefly then back to the crowd. "I will do all I can to make sure Arden is the last pack member stolen from us by this wretched curse. We're going to find Myrtle and Yvette and put an end to this cruelty. You have my word."

Hushed voices whisper words I can't hear, but I remain focused on Sutton. On the way he carries himself, the hope in his gaze as he looks out over his people. Then, he steps down, and chaos surrounds me.

People block my view of the stage, a sea of faces I don't recognize. "Serenity, it is so good to meet you." An elderly woman grips my hand. I don't recognize her, but she clearly knows who I am. "How did you like the jam?"

"I knew you would be good for this town." Another woman with white hair grips my other hand and beams at me like she's been the president of the Serenity Kellis fan club all along.

A man pushes in between the two women. "Arden would be happy to know you're still here with us."

"You helped us. Thank you."

"Thank you."

"Thank you so very much."

The words are repeated by dozens of voices. Sweat beads on my brow. It covers my palms while my heart races and spots invade my vision—all classic signs of a coming panic attack. I try to breathe, to suck in enough oxygen to calm my pulse, but the people just keep coming. I can't even hear them—not with the blood pounding in my ears.

"I need to find—"

Someone blocks my attempt to escape.

Until, finally, Sutton moves toward me, gaze hard. "Let's give Serenity some breathing room," he orders. The moment the words leave his lips, everyone backs off.

Hand on my elbow, he guides me smoothly through the crowd and outside. "Breathe," he orders as he leans me back against the side of the church.

I do, taking one deep breath after another. "They were everywhere."

"They don't know how to pace themselves," he says. "This is the first time we've ever had hope."

"I'm not the hero they think I am," I say, my voice cracking. "I'm a fucking journalist who lost her job because she got hammered when her fiancé cheated on her."

Sutton's gaze darkens. "You're a lot more than that, Serenity. And you'd damn well better figure that out sooner rather than later."

"What the hell do you think I'm trying to do?" I snap, regaining a bit of my composure. "I spent all day in your library, going through the books you pilfered from my stash. They hold nothing! Not a single fucking answer."

"Keep your voice down unless you want more company," he warns, his sharp tone more like the man I first met in the woods. The man who had more walls than Fort Knox.

Good.

If he shuts me out, it'll only make it easier to do the same to him.

"We're all going to die in this fucking town because you guys are relying on someone who knows nothing about magic or how to fight it."

His cheeks redden, his golden eyes glowing brightly. "We are not going to die here. And we certainly aren't only relying on you. Every single person here knows what's at stake because we've lived this reality for a century already. Every single year, someone has died, cementing our fate. Then you show up and things changed."

"You all got your wolves back, you mean. That could have been anything. Maybe she decided to give you that—"

"You can't believe she'd show mercy now. No, things changed—because of you, Serenity, regardless of what you choose to believe. What the hell is wrong with us having hope that you being here will change even more?" He steps back. "If you ask me, you're the dangerous one here because you refuse to see what's right in front of you."

My eyes fill with hot, angry tears, and I sniffle. "I'm the reason he's dead."

"If you want to blame yourself, then blame me too." He moves in closer, his voice dropping low. "Because I'm the one who was so desperate to taste you that I couldn't wait another moment. I'm the one who had his mouth on you in that library. So, if you're to blame, then so am I."

Lust burns in my belly at the not-so-distant memory he's awoken, and I can't help but let my gaze flicker to his lips despite the fact that we're standing outside a damned funeral surrounded by a crowd of mourners.

Because, I know that even with how scared I am

of failing, of what happens if we don't fix things, I want him.

I crave him.

And that wanting might very well get us both killed.

Clearing my throat, I push past him. "Fine, then we're both selfish assholes." Leaving him behind me, I push my way through the crowd, intent on heading for home. But when I see the woman standing on the steps, my thoughts of Sutton are forgotten for the moment.

Cara's expression is dark, her gaze hollow. She meets my eyes then looks away from me to someone over my shoulder.

"What is it?" Sutton questions from behind me.

"We found her."

I don't have to ask who she means. I know.

My breath catches.

"Where?" Sutton asks, moving to my side. I risk a glance at him, not at all surprised to see the change in his demeanor. He's tense, ready to spring, to fight.

"The eastern woods," Cara replies.

Sutton moves past her, taking my hand and pulling me along with him whether I want to go or not.

"Sutton," Cara says.

He spares her a glance. "What?"

She hesitates, her eyes on me again.

"If it's about Audrey, I want to know," I say.

"She should hear it," Sutton agrees.

Cara nods. "All right. Well, it's good news and bad news, I guess."

"Cara," Sutton warns.

He's running out of patience.

Cara's expression hardens. "Audrey's dead."

Chapter Five

I wouldn't exactly call my experience with death limited—I've seen my share of dead bodies—nor do I suffer from a weak stomach. But the sight of Audrey's decaying corpse nestled among layers of equally dead leaves is enough to make my gut churn threateningly. It isn't just the sagging, mushy skin draped over her bones like some kind of wet cloth. Nor is it the transparency of her flesh giving way to a clear view of the bone underneath. It's the fact that I can see nearly every inch of that skin—even the parts of her that really should have remained private.

I swallow hard against the urge to vomit right here where I stand in the middle of the woods.

"Serenity?" Sutton's voice is soft. Tentative. Like he's not sure if he'll spook me.

"What...happened?" I manage. "Why does she look like that?"

"This is what that bitch does," Cara says with distaste. "Every year, she outs herself at the ball, and then she chooses another unsuspecting victim to hide in. Audrey's not the first, and she won't be the last. I'd hoped to catch her before she did it again, but..." She frowns.

Sutton pats her on the shoulder. "We did our best, Cara."

Her words register with alarming clarity. Audrey's death is not a victory. It's only another loss.

"So, the witch used Audrey's body as a host," I say slowly.

Sutton nods. "The woman you met... That wasn't Audrey. Not really."

I shudder at the idea of it all. The witch is nothing more than a parasite taking over a host.

"I remember you mentioning this before, but I guess seeing it for myself is a different story."

"Audrey Fenrick has been dead for a year," he explains grimly. "The body was preserved because of the magic contained inside it. But when Myrtle left this body for the next, so did her magic. The decomposition reflects the time this host has been truly gone."

God. What a way to go. And now the witch, Myrtle, is walking around inside some other person, wearing their flesh like a twisted meat puppet.

But that still doesn't explain the nudity.

"What happened to her clothes?" I ask.

"Decomposed," Cara offers quietly.

Right.

Just like the rest of her.

I can't take it anymore; I look away.

"What should we do with her?" I hear Cara ask Sutton.

He gestures to the men we brought with us from the church. Pack members. He called them his security team, though I didn't catch their names before. Phineas is among them, and his gaze is hardened like the rest of them.

Instead of disgust, there is vengeance in their eyes.

I can't blame them.

Myrtle has taken so much from them.

I'd hate her too.

"We'll bury her," Sutton says quietly. "Here. I know it's not orthodox, but I don't think it's right to move her considering her condition. Put the word out. We'll do a small graveside service for anyone who wants to attend."

"I'll coordinate it," Phineas says. He pats his son's shoulder. "You have enough on your plate."

"Thanks," Sutton tells him.

Phineas motions to a couple of the security guys, and they all set to work clearing the brush so they can dig a grave.

I shudder.

Cara's head snaps up and she scans the trees.

"What is it?" Sutton asks.

"I don't know. I feel like something's out there," Cara murmurs.

Tensing, Sutton sweeps the forest, and I do the same, darting glances left and right. My heart thuds as I try not to think about who—or what—might be watching us.

"Check the perimeter," he says.

Cara nods and slips away, leaving us alone.

"Come on," he says, turning to me. "I should get you home. It'll be dark soon."

I grab Sutton's arm but hesitate to walk away, once again caught up in the nightmare that is Audrey's remains.

"What is it?" he asks.

"If she's not in there, where is she? Who is she?"

He hesitates, and I look up at him, only to realize it isn't uncertainty that gives him pause. He studies me like he's trying to decide if I can handle the answer. "She has always hidden among us," he says finally. "Taking the face and the body of one of our own. Audrey was only the most recent. And now, she has moved on."

Moved on.

My stomach tightens as I let his meaning settle over me. Audrey—Myrtle—is more than just a witch. She's a body stealer. A demon. A ghost.

No, not a ghost.

Something much worse than that. She's hiding in plain sight. She could literally be anyone.

As if he's thinking the same, Sutton glances at the security team, his worried gaze lingering on Phineas. "She could be any one of us now." His words so closely match my thoughts that I have to swallow the terror that rises. The knowledge that she is out there, wearing the skin of someone we trust, is far too terrifying a concept to be reality—but it is.

Real. All of this is real. A living nightmare, and we're all stuck inside it.

CARA DOESN'T FIND ANYTHING IN THE WOODS, BUT even so, Sutton insists on taking me home. I don't argue. Not when the alternative is to watch Phineas and the others bury a body that looks way overdue for being six feet under. He's quiet on the walk. So am I. All I can think of is Audrey Fenrick, the woman who became the face of a monster. She isn't Myrtle. I don't even know what Myrtle looks like. Not back then when she cast this horrible curse and not now that she's hiding inside another's body.

Yet, it's Audrey who will haunt my nightmares because she's the only face I can put on the monster we're up against. It's unfair to the kind woman she probably was before Myrtle sunk her claws into her. But I can't stop it.

The late afternoon sun slants in through the canopy overhead. It should have been a nice day. And it is as far as the weather. Somehow, the cheery sunshine makes my mood darker in contrast. Rain would be more appropriate. Or maybe a hurricane. I never knew sunshine to be so foreboding until I came to Midnight Falls, but it seems as if the sunnier it is, the deadlier things seem to get.

I stop suddenly, a horrifying thought suddenly hitting me.

"What is it?" Sutton asks.

He looks from me to the woods around us as if my senses somehow trump his. I look at him with wide eyes. His worry is sliced raw, and I can't blame him after the day we've both had. But I have to know.

"If Myrtle has stolen another body, that means whoever she's chosen is dead now too."

He sighs, his shoulders sagging. "Yes."

He doesn't say anything else. Neither do I. What is there to say? Someone we know is dead, and we can't even mourn them.

When he takes my hand, I let him, though I can barely feel it through the numbness that has descended like a coating over my skin. Death. That's what I've witnessed since coming to this town. The familiar guilt threatens to override my apathy, seeping in through the cracks in my armor.

Tears well in my tired eyes.

By the time we reach the house, the grief has settled on my shoulders, weighing me down until the world itself seems like it's resting on my back.

Sutton holds the door to let me pass and then

shuts it behind us with a slam hard enough to knock some plaster loose.

The sound jars me, and I jerk toward it—and him. "What was that for?"

"Apologies," he says, though his tone is too snide to be genuine. "I'm losing my patience with this performance of yours."

My jaw hangs open until I can find the words. "You call reacting to three deaths in one day a *performance*?"

"Three deaths," he agrees, "And none of them were your own. Yet, you're acting like you're already gone."

"I'm not *acting*," I say through clenched teeth. "Or performing. I'm feeling. Pardon me if I'm processing in two days what you've had a century to accept."

He runs a hand through his hair, his eyes a bit wild now. "Maybe you're right. Maybe you deserve more time. But, dammit, we don't have that luxury. You might be willing to ignore what you feel for me, Serenity, but I care too damn much about you to watch you go down this path."

"And what path is that?" My voice rises.

This asshole has some nerve.

"The one where you give up without a fight."

We're both yelling now. I'm not sure when my temper eclipsed my sadness, but the fire in my veins is a welcome feeling after so much grief and guilt. It brings a clarity I lacked before. He's right, I realize. I had given up, or nearly, though I refuse to admit that now that he's being an ass about it.

"I'm doing my best, Sutton. The problem is— what I'm capable of and what this town thinks I can do for them are two wildly different things."

"You're wrong," he says quietly.

He might not be yelling, but his words still get under my skin.

"How can you be so damned sure?"

"Because I've known since before I met you that you're—"

He breaks off, clearly not willing to finish, but with a beginning like that, I'm just getting warmed up.

"Before you met me? What the hell does that mean?"

"Nothing. Look, it's been a long day. Get some sleep. Take some time."

"If you tell me to relax or calm down, I swear, Sutton, the next dead body in this town will be yours."

He sighs though it almost sounds like a growl.

I've irritated him. Good. He's confused and infuriated me.

"What do you mean, 'before you met me'?" I repeat.

I don't expect him to answer me. Not with the argument we've just had. So when he starts telling me the story, I forget to be mad and instead get caught up in the tale. "Six months ago, I met a woman in the forest near this house. A witch named Rina. She's a bit of a gypsy, no coven, no family." He snorts at some memory. "I very nearly killed her, thanks to my own prejudices against her kind. But she eventually earned my trust, and we became friends for a time."

Despite it having no place here, jealousy stabs through me. What kind of friends, exactly, were they?

"How did she earn your trust?"

"She performed a blood augury."

"A blood what?"

"Augury. What you would call a spell, though it's more of a divination."

"I see."

Actually, I don't. Not really. The more I hear about it, the more complicated the idea of magic seems.

"And what did this augury show you that made you trust this Rina woman so much?"

Is it wrong to hate someone without ever meeting her? Because my hormones kind of want to stake a claim I have no right to make right now. Whoever she is, she's not good enough for Sutton, that's for damn sure.

"The point of an augury is to answer a question. You can ask anything you want." He hesitates and then adds, "I asked her to give me the name of the witch powerful enough to stop Myrtle and break this curse."

My mind empties. Jealousy is replaced by anxiety. My heart pounds. I stare at Sutton, not sure I want to hear the rest, but I can't walk away now. I have to know.

"And?" I say on a whisper, my eyes searching his. The answer is clear in his gaze before it ever passes over his lips.

"The name she gave me was yours."

Shock, disbelief; a hundred arguments, and even more excuses land on my tongue. In my throat. Squeezing my chest until my heart constricts. "It can't be."

But I already know it is. Or that he's not lying, at least. Whatever he saw, this blood augury he witnessed ended with me. That much is clear from the way he stares at me now.

"I saw it for myself," he says quietly, and while he speaks, my memory takes me back to that first day in the woods. He'd been shocked to see me on his side of the boundary line, but that surprise had been short-lived. He'd known then who I was. Or what.

"Were you the one who sent the newspaper articles to my apartment?"

Hot anger works its way into my veins. The very idea that he's been lying to me this whole time is a wrong I can't imagine making right—

"What articles?"

His confusion is convincing enough alone, but the sharp worry that follows is undeniable.

"Serenity, did someone from this town contact you before you came here?"

"Yes. And they made sure I knew just enough to want to investigate. They knew me," I add, realizing with stark clarity how true that is. They knew I was a journalist, one with nothing left to lose. Why else would I have come in the first place?

They gave me just enough information to hook me. But not enough to know how dangerous it would be to even try.

Sutton's brows furrow, and I know from the look he wears—a look that suggests he might just kill whoever it was—that it wasn't him.

"I believe you," I say. He doesn't answer, clearly waiting for me to decide how I feel about this information. After a beat of silence, I add, "And you're really sure your friend wasn't wrong about me?"

"A witch can lie, but blood cannot," he adds. "You are the key to breaking this curse, Serenity. And the sooner you accept that, the better we'll all be for it."

Chapter Six

Sutton insists on walking me upstairs. Inside the bedroom, I turn to face him, wanting only to be alone, and brace myself for an argument. But he's already heading out again. His shoulders are a bit hunched, but he doesn't push me, not about what he just admitted.

"Where are you going?" I ask, unwilling to admit a big part of me wants him to stay. More than that. I want him to strip this dress off my body and love me so completely there's no room left for the fear and uncertainty I feel now. But a love like that scares me almost as much as learning I'm a witch.

What I feel for Sutton Hargrave is beautiful and terrifying.

"I'm going to make some dinner."

I blink, surprised to hear his answer includes something so normal as preparing a meal. But I should have known. Sutton's always been good at taking care of me.

"Sutton," I call before he can disappear down the stairs.

When he turns back, stormy emotions swirl in his dark gaze. I clasp my hands together to keep from reaching out to him. To run my hands over the lapels of his jacket. To bury them in his hair.

"Thank you for being honest," I say, my voice barely above a whisper.

He studies me, the intensity in his eyes sucking all the air out of the room. My breaths are shallow, and my heart thuds so loudly I'm sure he can hear it. The silence stretches, and I can feel my control slipping. Any longer and I'll give in to the urge to let him comfort me.

I turn away, staring blindly out the window. "I'll be down soon."

I don't look up until the sound of his footsteps has faded down the stairs.

Alone, I hurry to the door and push it closed. My fingers fumble with the dress, and suddenly, I can't get it off fast enough. The lace is a reminder of everything that's happened today. I want it gone.

I'm just pulling a sweatshirt on over leggings when my phone rings. The shrill sound of it makes me jump. Allison's name flashes on the screen. I grab it off the bed, answering quickly to silence the sound.

"Hello?" I do my best to force cheer into my voice.

"How are things in Smallville?" Allison jokes into the line.

"Peachy. What's up?"

"You okay?"

I try harder to coat my words with false cheer. "Fine." Settling onto the bed, I lean back against Sutton's headboard and tuck my knees to my chest. "How are you?"

"Great. Had a date last night, was horrible. Dude talked about cats all night."

"Cats?"

"Yes. And we're not even talking about the animals. He's obsessed with the musical."

I snort out a genuine half-laugh, a sound that is alien to me in my current state. "Hey, I like it too. My grandmother and I used to watch it once a year."

"Okay, but did you have special bed sheets made with the faces of your favorite felines?"

"No, he didn't."

"Yes, yes he did."

I let myself be distracted by the easy conversation, a nice break from the dark reality that has descended on me like a truckload of bricks. "Wait, how do you know what kind of sheets he has?"

Allison groans. "Don't slut shame, Ser. It's been forever, and he was really, *really* hot, especially when he stopped talking."

I shake my head, in no way judging. Hell, I wish I could have a quick roll in the sheets. Might help me get my head right. The image of Sutton above me, of his hands on my body, assaults my mind and I shove it away. "No judgment here, trust me." Only jealousy. "Was the sex at least good?"

"Guy is bendy, I'll tell you that much. I might be seeing him again later."

"You get that kitty some catnip," I joke.

Allison falls silent, her lack of words telling me there's more to the reason she called than to discuss hot sex with cat-man.

"Out with it, already."

She sighs into the line. "Quincy hired someone for your position today."

Her words are yet another blow. And it's just not today either. One after the other, they've been coming since the day Roscoe dumped me in the middle of that stupid restaurant. My hand tightens on the phone. How many more hits am I supposed to take before I just stay the hell down?

And then it hits me. I've *been* down. Whether I realized it or not, I got knocked over the night of that ball, and I've been staying on the ground ever since. But that shit ends now. Myrtle may not be who called me here in the first place, but she's the one who has trapped me. Because of her, I can't go back and see my family. Can't return to the *Times* and demand my job back. Can't take that Mexico vacation with my best friend that I promised her I would.

Myrtle stole my life. And it's well past time I took it back.

"Serenity?"

"That really sucks," I reply.

"It does. But you'll get it back. You're still working on that story, right?"

"I am."

Am I? Is Midnight Falls a story I'll write? Something about the idea feels too much like crossing a boundary.

"It has to stay a secret though," I add. "Steven is insisting I come home, and I can't. Not yet."

"Always the stubborn-ass," she replies, and I can hear the smile in her tone.

"Always and forever," I retort. "Thanks for letting me know about the job. I'll find a way to get it back when I'm done here."

Even as I say the words, I'm not sure I believe them anymore. Or that I care. It unsettles me. Working for the Times was my dream. If that dream is gone, what do I have left?

"That's my girl," Allison says proudly.

"Now, go have crazy sex with cat-man," I tell her, and she laughs.

"Cat man? Really? That sounds like a superhero name. Though, given what he did to me last night, it's fitting—"

"Save the details for brunch when I get home. Love your face, bitch."

"You too."

With renewed purpose, I end the call and toss the phone to the bed beside me. I've never been one to give up or wallow in self-pity. And without real- izing it, that's exactly what I've been doing since Roscoe dumped me.

Wallowing. Which is absolutely pathetic. I got hammered, let my responsibilities slip, blamed Quincy for giving my story away, and then ran away. I was chasing a story, yes, but running none-theless. But no damn more. From this moment on, I'm going to stop running. Instead, I'm going to turn around and face my problems head-on. Starting with what I feel for Sutton Hargrave.

———

AN HOUR LATER, HAIR STILL WET FROM MY GET-your-shit-together shower, I open the bedroom door and step into the hall. The moment I do, I'm hit with an absolutely mouthwatering aroma. Following it, I descend the stairs and head into the kitchen.

At the bottom of the steps, I round the corner—and halt.

My heart hammers as I take in the scene before me. Sutton has covered the table in a black cloth and placed two candlesticks on top. A flame flickers atop each one. It's romantic as hell, and when Sutton turns to me, I know I'm a goner. He's wearing a fucking apron, and for some reason, I'm instantly turned on. Who knew I liked my men domestic? Or maybe it's the fact that the wildness in him is only ever tamed for me. Either way, Sutton Hargrave in a white apron is pure sex.

"Figured you might be hungry." Using a spatula,

he lifts a steak from the skillet and sets it on a plate. Then, he scoops some potatoes out of a large pot and puts them beside it.

My stomach growls, and Sutton grins. Apparently, the way to my heart is through food—and Sutton's already figured it out.

"What are we having?" I ask, working hard to keep my voice neutral.

"Garlic butter steaks and mashed potatoes."

Fuck it, that's it. I'm going to marry this former murder suspect. "That sounds amazing."

"Glad to hear it. Mable brought the groceries, and, well, it's been a while since I've been able to cook a steak. Usually, my meat consists of—" He stops and grimaces. "We don't need to get into that."

He sets my plate down and pulls out the chair.

Grateful he left out something that might have ruined my appetite, I move toward him and take a seat at the table. He helps me scoot my chair back in then heads back into the kitchen to retrieve his own dinner.

I study him as he comes back carrying his plate and a bottle of red wine. He takes a seat to my left, not across from me, and pours the crimson liquid into my glass.

"Were you able to rest?" he asks.

I eye him, knowing full well his werewolf hearing picked up on my conversation with Allison. But he gives nothing away, clearly intent on preserving my sense of privacy.

"A bit," I reply, watching him curiously. *What the hell caused this shift?* Less than an hour ago, he was pissed at me. Hell, I was pissed at him too.

When he's filled his own glass, I take a sip of the wine, savoring the heavy flavor as it dances on my tongue. "Actually, my friend Allison called me. Apparently, she had epic sex with a cat-man last night."

Sutton chokes on his wine, and I grin.

"I'm sorry, she what?" he asks.

"He is obsessed with the musical Cats." When Sutton continues to stare at me, I shake my head. "He's not an actual cat-man," I tell him. "Just wishes he was."

"That is … interesting."

"It is. The whole no-strings thing is something I miss." The words are out before I realize their implication.

Sutton doesn't miss it though. He stares at me, his hazel gaze locking on mine. "Oh?"

My cheeks heat, and I'm forced to backpedal.

"Not that I've had a lot of no-strings relationships. Honestly, that's how things started with Roscoe. I guess I shouldn't have been surprised when he fucked his paralegal behind my back."

Sutton's mood shifts, the energy in the room shifting with him as he sets his wine glass down.

"I'm sorry. I shouldn't be rambling. Especially not when you made us such a great dinner." I lift my fork and knife and slice off a piece of steak. Slipping it into my mouth, I nearly groan as the explosion of flavor overtakes my senses. "Oh my gosh, this is delicious," I manage as soon as I've swallowed. I take another bite and then a third before I realize Sutton isn't eating. He's watching me. "Eat, Sutton. Please. You're missing out."

"I disagree. Watching you is not missing out on anything."

Heat rushes between my legs. Because I know what kind of pleasure he is capable of granting me, it's easy to imagine him throwing this entire table aside and doing it all over again right here. Right now. The idea of letting him have me for dessert hangs between us.

But he doesn't move toward me, and I can't decide if I'm relieved or disappointed.

"Please eat," I say with a half-hearted smile.

"It's been a long time since you've had steak, remember? And you were so excited."

"It's been a long time since I've had a lot of things," he replies, "as you so generously pointed out just the other night." He retrieves his fork and knife and begins to cut himself a bite. With controlled movements, he spears the steak and puts it into his mouth.

Now, it's my turn to watch him, and I can't even be bothered to care that the way the man eats turns me on. The way he breathes. Takes a drink. Honestly, Sutton Hargrave breathing is a thing of beauty. And with that realization, I lift my glass and down my wine.

The buzz doesn't even touch my lust. Honestly, it makes it worse because the alcohol blurs the line drawn between us, making it damn near impossible to remember why it is such a bad idea.

Sutton sets his silverware down and grips the table. "Serenity." My name is a plea, though for what, I cannot be sure.

"What?"

"I can sense it," he says, tone strained as if he's barely leashing the animal inside.

Is it bad I want to let it free? We're trapped here. Why can't we have something casual? Something like Allison has? A bit of life when we're surrounded by so much death?

"Sense what?" I ask, my voice hoarse. I may already know the answer, and taunting him may be wrong, but I can't help it. I want to hear it.

He turns to me, his gaze brighter now, almost shimmering with gold. "The way I make you feel."

I swallow hard and clench my thighs together, trying like hell to ease the throbbing between them. "We—"

"We what?" he asks, slowly getting to his feet.

Uh-oh.

"We shouldn't..." I trail off as he drops to his knees and scoots my chair back. "I don't know if this is a good idea," I manage as he slips between my legs and braces his hands on either side of my chair.

Sutton leans in. "Then why do you smell like you want me to bury myself in you? Like you want my hands on your body? My mouth on your skin?"

Fuckballs. "Because I can't think straight when I'm around you."

"Why is that, I wonder?"

Umm, because you're fucking sexy? Because you brought me more pleasure in five minutes than Roscoe did in all the years we were together?

Because my hormones want me to mount you right here, right now? "I can't think of anything," I lie.

Sutton grins because the truth is my body has already betrayed me. Since I didn't have any underwear, my leggings are soaked completely through, and given his ability to sense things—I know he knows it too.

"What would you do if I touched you right now?" he asks.

Come apart. "I don't know."

"No?" As if to test a theory, he reaches out and runs a finger along my jaw. I shiver, his finger lighting a fire along my skin. "You want me, Serenity, the same way I want you. Why are you holding back? It has to be more than wanting to focus."

"Why?"

"Because we have nothing to focus on now. So, tell me, what is it?"

I meet his gaze, and my honesty makes my voice raw. "I don't know."

That does it. Sutton snaps. In the span of a heartbeat, his hand snakes around my neck and he slams his mouth to mine. My hands go to his hair then his shoulders and I grip him, throwing myself out of the chair and onto his body. We tumble to the floor, landing with me on top of him as his tongue slips into my mouth.

His kiss is a claiming, and I've never wanted anything more.

Straddling him, my hands go to his waist, gripping his shirt and ripping it up so I can feel his warm flesh against my fingertips. I grind down against his hard length, moaning as it presses against me. He rolls us over and thrusts against me.

The clothes between us have never felt more like a prison.

Sutton is savage as he fucks my mouth with his tongue. Taking. Tasting. And I'm just as damned wild. Because right now, in this moment, I want him inside of me more than I want to draw my next breath.

He reaches down and tears my shirt open then drops his mouth to my exposed breast. I arch up into him, crying out as he gently sucks and nips, his nimble fingers expertly toying with my other breast. I let my hands trail down to the fly of his jeans, and I undo the button, slip my hand inside, and grip the hard length of him.

He growls, the sound vibrating against my skin, and I squeeze gently before stroking him. He pumps into my hand, one thrust, two, before taking my mouth again with a hungry growl.

I was wrong before. Being with Sutton isn't something I need to deny myself. Not if I can do it on my terms. Nothing this good can be that bad. Right?

Something shifts inside of me, an energy I don't recognize, and before I can pull away, a flash of blue fills the room, and Sutton is thrown from my body. Chest rising and falling in heavy succession, he stares at me from where he's landed against the wall, eyes wild and knowing.

I don't speak.

Don't move.

"My magical gift is apparently a cock-block." My bleak attempt at a joke is not met with a smile from Sutton, though he does crawl back over to me so we're sitting a few feet from each other. "If that was magic," I add.

"It was," he replies.

"Why? Why does that happen whenever we... And why didn't it happen the night of the party?"

He shakes his head. "I don't know. But it had better kill me the next time it interrupts us."

I take a deep breath, trying to get control of

myself now that the damned blue spark has thrown yet another cold bucket of water on the two of us.

Though, this time, it cemented my resolve. Solidified my purpose.

I am going to stop Myrtle.

Fix this town.

Free myself.

Get my job back.

And I'm *going* to get the chance to experience what Sutton and I can be together.

Because what I feel for him is far too potent to not try.

Chapter Seven

T he following day, I agree to attend a pack meeting. Sutton does a terrible job at hiding his pleasure when I say yes. Even Phineas is exuberant. You'd think I already broke the curse, considering their light moods as we walk to town. More than once, I catch Sutton's gaze on me, and I can't help but wonder if he's still thinking about last night. Just the memory of how he felt against me heats my skin. I'm not sure whether to be ashamed of the fact that my determination to master my magic stems just as much from wanting Sutton as it does from wanting to stop Myrtle.

It's why I've agreed to come today.

So I can *come* tomorrow, so to speak. Even as I

think it, the image of me looking down at Sutton comes to mind, only overpowered by the memory of him rolling us over and grinding into me like—

"Serenity?"

"Huh?" I glance at both Phineas and Sutton, who are watching me, concern reflected in their gazes. "Did you hear me?" Phineas asks.

Shit. "Sorry, I was distracted."

"You feeling all right?" Phineas asks.

Sutton's knowing grin makes me blush. Thankfully, though, he lets it go.

I force a smile, grateful Phineas doesn't seem to be picking up on the fact that I am in a constant state of 'turned the fuck on' whenever I'm near Sutton. "Fine. Just tired." *And imagining having sex with your son,* I add silently because doing so out loud would be awkward.

Besides, add that to my lack of sleep last night, and I figure I've got a pretty damn good reason for being distracted. After getting my shit together and resolving to not wallow in self-pity anymore, I laid awake half the night, trying to come up with some plan that doesn't involve me facing off with a witch whose ability and knowledge of magic surpasses mine by at least a century. But nothing else comes to mind. Not while I have no idea whose body she's hiding in, anyway.

She could literally be anyone at this point. Which makes priority number one to learn more about this magic I somehow unknowingly possess and figure out what it makes me capable of.

At some point, I'd even given up on sleeping and crept down to the library where I scoured the pages of books I'd already read. Anything with local legends or any mention of witches. Sutton found me there early this morning. He'd walked in carrying a croissant and coffee, wearing nothing but a pair of low-slung sweatpants.

It's a good thing Phineas walked in behind him. Otherwise, I might have tried for round two right there on the desk, magic sparks be damned.

That blue spark is giving me lady blue balls, and I don't appreciate it.

"We were just brainstorming ideas about where Yvette might be hiding," Phineas says.

"Are we sure she's not hiding in another body too?" I ask.

The moment the words are out, I regret them. Speculating on something like that only adds to our problems. Sutton and Hargrave exchange a glance.

"In a hundred years, Myrtle's been the only one to steal a host," Sutton says.

"Things are changing," Phineas says, clearly not as convinced as Sutton.

"True," he agrees reluctantly.

"I don't think Yvette is quite as powerful as her sister," I say, thinking back to the tree she uprooted the last time we were at the bed and breakfast together. If she were as powerful as Myrtle, she wouldn't have missed me.

"What does the pack say?" Phineas asks.

"A lot of them are angry with themselves," Sutton admits.

"For what?" I ask, surprised.

"For never figuring out Myrtle and Yvette are sisters," Sutton explains.

"That isn't their fault," I say. "Besides, what matters now is finding them."

"If she can't steal a host body, Yvette will be easier to find," Phineas says. He glances from me to Sutton. "She can't have gone far from her place of business, don't you think?"

"I'm not sure I'm the best person to ask," I say with a shrug. "You two know this town better than I do."

"Yes, but you lived under the same roof with her," Phineas points out just as we pass very nearby the Bed and Breakfast in question, and I shudder.

"Don't remind me," I say, refusing to look up at the imposing Victorian house I once thought was cute and cozy. Since the night of the ball, it's been under constant surveillance from the pack. Yvette hasn't shown her face once, but anytime someone tries to enter, some sort of invisible barrier blocks their attempt.

The place is magically locked up tight. Either she's holed up inside or she hopes to return; no one knows which.

"We'll think of something," Sutton says, and I can see he doesn't like the idea of me being involved in any way where Yvette is concerned.

The feeling is mutual.

"What we should be discussing is how we're going to narrow down our list of suspects," I say. "If Myrtle could be anyone, that gives us an entire town's worth of people to investigate." I look at Phineas apologetically.

"I know, that includes me," he says.

"Dad, come on," Sutton says.

"He's right," I say. "Until we know for sure,

everyone's a suspect. Myrtle's chosen men just as often as women over the years."

Sutton scowls. He doesn't argue, but I can tell he wants to. The truth is I've already been alone with Phineas twice since the night of the ball, which has already given him more than enough chances to make a move. But I have to look at this like a true investigator would. Without emotion or bias. Because there's no room for either when it's a matter of life or death.

"Fine," Sutton says begrudgingly. "We'll bring it up at the meeting."

"Talk to Mable. She's always been the one to head that up for us." Phineas gestures at the building just ahead, and I realize we've arrived.

The church is already crowded, and being back here so soon after the funeral turns my stomach. I can still visualize the casket up at the front, hear the muted sobs of the people in the pews. I doubt it's a memory I'll ever forget.

We pause in the vestibule while Sutton greets people. Through the open doors, I see pack members I recognize from the funeral, as well as some I don't, gathered inside the cramped sanctuary. The pews are packed full of bodies with the overflow crowding in against the walls on both sides.

I take a deep, steadying breath to calm my nerves and remind myself of my decision. No wallowing. No hiding. *Serenity Kellis doesn't run.*

Phineas goes in first, but before I can follow, Sutton grabs my wrist.

"What's wrong?" I ask quietly.

"Just... Stay close," he says.

"If there's a threat, just tell me—"

"She could be any of them," he says, and I stiffen, realizing he's right.

There's a very good chance one of the people inside these walls is Myrtle, and I'm not about to make myself an easy target. Not again.

"You too," I say and then head inside, heart in my throat.

I make it as far as the sanctuary doors before people begin to recognize me. They press in closer, shaking my hand, hugging me, patting my arms. Every one of them carries a familiar glint in their eye: hope. It's unnerving. And way too much even for my newfound determination.

I hesitate, unsure about continuing if it means enduring this kind of attention. But then Sutton is at my back, his warmth pushing me onward. At a single word from him, the crowd moves aside for us.

I make my way down the center aisle, eyes on Phineas, who waits at the front. In the front row, Mable gestures for me to sit beside her. I sink down, grateful for friendly faces.

Sutton watches to be sure I'm settled and then makes his way to the front. Rather than demand silence, he simply stands at the podium and waits for them to give it.

"Thanks for coming," he says when the room quiets. "I know many of you have already heard, but we found remains yesterday that belong to the late Audrey Fenrick."

The room fills with hushed conversations. When I turn to glance at the rows behind me, their uncertain gazes are sweeping the room. They're just as uneasy as I am about the implication.

Sutton holds up a hand. "I know we all understand what this means."

"If she isn't Audrey, she's one of us," someone says. He stands, and I recognize George, the grumpy cashier at the drug store where I bought my phone charger. He still looks just as salty as he did the day I met him, except now, I can't really fault him for it.

"You have every right to be concerned," Sutton says. "But this is something we go through every year—"

"That's where you're wrong," George snaps. "*We* go through this shit every year. Find a body. Clean it up. Wait for the next one. Meanwhile, you just sit up in your mansion and bide your time until the next party. And now you're here, trying to order us around like we haven't been already doin' this shit for a century."

I tense, waiting for Sutton's inevitable reaction. But he simply nods. "You're right, George. Thanks to the curse, I've been unable to help you all until now."

George scowls, and I wonder if he's disappointed he didn't get the reaction he wanted from his alpha. Honestly, it's for the best. I've no doubt Sutton could rip him apart before George could so much as howl.

Sutton's calm, quiet gaze sweeps the crowd. "The curse punished us all because Myrtle wanted to punish me. We've all paid the price, and maybe I've been away too long. In my absence, you've been forced to lead yourselves. To pick up the pieces of Myrtle's horrific actions every year."

"Yeah, and maybe that shouldn't change."

George's tone is icy now. It pisses me off. I start to stand, but a voice in the crowd stops me.

"Bull shit." From across the aisle, Cara stands, glaring at George before turning back to Sutton. "Don't let George get in your head. He's grouchy from not getting laid last year because he was too afraid Myrtle was using the body of Fred Gordon's wife, which meant he couldn't use it for himself if you know what I mean."

A few gasps sounded.

"Uh-oh," Mable mutters under her breath.

"Now, you just wait a damn minute," George begins. "First of all, my personal life ain't none of your business."

Another man stands up, eyes narrowed at George. "Are you saying it's true?" he demands.

"That's Fred Gordon," Mable whispers. "And his wife Sylvia."

Obviously. My gaze shifts to the flushed brunette woman with her hands folded tightly in her lap. She doesn't look up, doesn't make eye contact with anyone.

George doesn't answer, which only seems to make Fred angrier.

Fred's hands ball into fists. "You were sleeping with my wife?" The woman beside him on the bench literally sinks a few inches in her seat, still refusing to meet anyone's eye.

"Well, not in the last year anyway," Cara says wryly, and I have to press my lips together to keep from laughing at her candor.

Beside me, Mable seems like she's trying to keep it together too. She takes my hand and squeezes, and I wonder if she's comparing this scandal to an episode of Bridgerton in her head.

"Look, all I'm saying is ever since that woman came to town, nothing's been safe." George looks at me, and my smile vanishes. "After she got here, Myrtle stepped up her game, and now, supposedly Yvette is a damned witch too."

"*Supposedly?*" Cara echoes. "Are you saying you don't believe it?"

"I'm saying the only people whose word we have to go on is that outsider over there." George points a stabbing finger in my direction, and the entire room fixes me with their stares. "And the man she's fucking. Our supposed alpha."

I search for the right words, but it turns out I don't need to have any. In the silence that follows, a roar fills the room, so loud it shakes the rafters. The floor booms with the weight of Sutton's body as he leaps from the stage and strides down the aisle.

George doesn't have time to move before Sutton grabs him by the shirt and hauls him into the air, growling into the man's face. "Watch your mouth, asshole," Sutton snarls at him. "You want to challenge me for alpha, you go ahead. We'll take this outside and settle it here and now. Otherwise, you bite your tongue, and do not speak her name again unless it is with respect."

Sutton lets go of George and turns slowly, eyeing the crowded room. "I know you've all been left alone, cut off from the rest of the world, but I've been more alone than anyone in this town has a right to claim. And still, I come, and I fight for you. With you. I am your alpha, and if you want to change that, you will challenge me and take it." He looks over at George, who's climbing unsteadily to his feet from where Sutton unceremoniously dropped him on his ass. "Until then, we keep fighting the real enemy instead of each other."

George doesn't argue.

"Well, now that we've gotten that out of the way," Cara says dryly, "Can we talk about the actual bitch we're here to kill instead of acting like one ourselves?"

I bite my lip to keep from cracking up. The look

on her face means business, and no one questions her. I can't blame them.

Sutton returns to the front where Cara waits impatiently.

"Well, alpha?" she says pointedly. "What are we doing to hunt these two psycho sisters down?"

Others murmur what sounds like their agreement to her question. I look at them then her and realize it's Cara who's been holding all this together while Sutton's been away. At some point in all this, she took the reins. And now she's just handed them right back over to him.

My respect for her grows immensely. It takes great strength to step up when the world is falling apart. And even greater strength to know when to return the power granted during chaos.

Sutton returns to the podium.

His eyes linger on mine a moment before he clears his throat and answers her question. "Now that we're able to shift again, we have senses and strengths we didn't have before. That means we have an advantage we didn't have before too. We've upped the patrols and are doing everything we can to scour every inch of this town for any sign of either one of them."

"How does that help if we don't know who she

is?" someone calls. One of the guys from Sutton's security team yesterday. He's not arguing like George, but he looks worried. "She could literally be any one of us."

"You're right, Vaughn," Sutton says grimly. "But we have to be smart. That means not going anywhere alone. Groups of three are best, actually. More when you can."

Murmurs of agreement go around. They already have a pack mentality, I realize. For some reason, it makes the gifts they've sent me seem less crazy. More flattering. Neighbors who are also a wolf pack; you don't get more tightly-knit than that, and here they are, welcoming me in knowing I'm just as much a suspect as they are. I turn my head just enough to spot George glowering in the crowd. Well, *most* of them are welcoming.

"It's only a start, but we can't forget how far we've come already," Sutton goes on, gaining steam as his pep talk seems to gain traction. His confidence and determination are contagious. I can see it in the way they watch him, nodding at his words. "Getting our wolves back. Bringing down the wall between town and the manor house." His eyes flick to me, but he doesn't say my name, and I'm grateful for it. He looks back at the crowd. "We have Myrtle and Yvette on the run, and we have each other. Wherever Myrtle is, whoever she is, she knows we aren't going to wait another year to hunt her down. This ends now. And she knows it."

When he finishes, the crowd cheers.

Their energy pumps adrenaline through me until I can barely catch my breath just sitting here in the front pew. For a wild moment, I believe him. Just like they do. That we'll find her in time. That we'll uncover a way to beat her at this macabre game she's forced us to play. That we'll be free.

And it's exhilarating. Sutton himself is inspiring. I can see why they follow him.

When the room quiets again, Sutton talks about logistics and reminders about not being alone if possible. He calls Mable to the podium, and she rattles off something about initiating "suspect protocol," which, from what I can tell, is a process involving everyone registering at the library for some sort of interrogation process they've developed from past years of narrowing down suspect lists. I'm impressed, though I'm not sure whether I should be since it hasn't seemed to work before.

Still, at least, they're trying.

After that, Sutton calls for more volunteers for patrols as well as anyone interested in taking the Sheriff's position to please contact him, and the meeting begins to break up. Most people leave, and I find myself sitting alone on the bench while Sutton and Mable coordinate all of their plans.

"Hey." Cara sits down beside me. "How are you holding up?"

"I'm not sure," I admit.

She smirks. "Honesty, I like it."

"In that case, full honesty? Life is really fucking weird lately."

She snorts and spreads her arms wide. "Welcome to Midnight Falls."

I can't help but laugh at that. So accurate.

"Hey, listen," I say, the humor fading way too fast as reality sets in again. "Thanks for everything you said earlier. Standing up for Sutton—"

"No thanks necessary. He's a great alpha. Being trapped away from us hasn't changed that. I know he would have been here if he could have."

"Well, I appreciate it. And everything you're doing out there with the patrols and searches. You finding Audrey..."

"It's no big deal," she says. When she sees my face, she shakes her head, rueful. "Okay, it was a big deal. Disgusting, actually. But it's also nice to just be doing wolf things again. Shifting, running, tracking—I've missed it so damn much."

"I can't imagine," I say quietly.

She studies me. "Listen, I know everyone's pressuring you about all this." She glances around the room, now nearly empty, thankfully, and I look away. "But don't let them get in your head."

"Too late," I mutter, and when I look up, empathy is written all over her face.

"Oh, girlfriend, you're a mess, aren't you?" I don't have a chance to answer—not that she can't see it clearly written on my face—before she adds, "That's it. Girls' night out. You and me. Tonight."

"Wait, seriously?"

"Do I look like I joke about stuff like ladies' nights?"

"No, but... There's so much going on."

"If there's one thing I've learned about living in this damned cursed town, it's that our problems will still be there tomorrow."

I sigh. She's not wrong.

Sutton catches my eye, and even though Mable's still talking, he nods at me. I realize with a start that he can actually hear our conversation way over here. And he's telling me to say yes.

Maybe Cara's right.

And after what she did earlier, siding with Sutton as alpha, she's officially been crossed off my suspect list. No way would Myrtle argue for Sutton keeping his power. Besides, a night away from it all sounds too good to pass up.

"Okay," I say, smiling. "I'm in."

"Hell yeah, you are," she says. "And no talk of witches or wolves at all, deal?"

I smile gratefully. "Deal."

Chapter Eight

"You're going out like that?" Sutton all but chokes out when I make it downstairs. As uncomfortable as I was with the dress Cara dropped off for me earlier—which is short enough to qualify as a shirt, honestly—the look on Sutton's face makes every missing inch of fabric worth it.

A shimmering blue, it barely covers my ass, and to top it off, I've actually taken the time to style my hair and put some makeup on my face. I feel like a new woman. "I am. Is that a problem?" Turning, I bend over and slip into my shoes.

Sutton growls, the predatory sound shooting straight through me. Suddenly, the evening I was looking forward to doesn't seem so great because I know, without a doubt, Sutton and I would have far more fun staying in.

"You're going to kill me," he snarls.

I turn around. Eyes so bright they're practically glowing, he stands less than three feet from me now, both hands clenched into fists. "Considering you're immortal, I can't say I'm all that concerned," I reply.

He actually looks pained as he does his best to collect himself and say, "You look stunning."

"That's more of what I was looking for."

He takes a step toward me, and the doorbell rings. "I'm going to kill whoever is on the other side of that door."

"I'd really rather you didn't," Cara calls from outside.

Chuckling, I pull it open to see she's not wearing much more than I am. In fact, she's wearing less. A crop top bares her midsection while a skirt the length of mine sits low on her hips. She's styled her pixie-cut hair into short spikes, massively embracing the whole Tinkerbell look. "You look awesome."

"So do you." She winks then turns to Sutton. "I'll have her back by one."

He doesn't respond, gaze still on me.

"He's going to stand there all night if we don't leave," I joke.

"Then let's get going." Cara turns and heads down the porch steps, so I move toward the door. Before I can get there, though, Sutton snakes an arm around my waist and yanks me back against his body. The feel of him pressed against me—

"Waiting for you to get home is going to be torture." His breath fans over my neck as he speaks.

Home. His word slams into me with much more strength than I'm sure he intended. I hadn't even realized it, but Sutton's house *does* feel like home to me. Shit—we are living together. When the hell did that happen? I swallow hard. "I'll be back soon enough. Besides, you could probably use a break from me."

I pull away and turn to face him.

"Never."

I suck in a breath at the intensity of his stare and force myself to turn away and join Cara outside before I do something stupid and rip his clothes off. Then again, maybe that's not so stupid...

"You ready?" Cara asks, pulling me back to reality.

"I am."

"Great."

Minutes tick by in silence as we make our way to town, wearing shoes that should never be worn in the woods. But without a driveway, Sutton's house is not accessible any other way.

"You okay?" Cara questions as the town lights come into view ahead.

"I'm good."

"Thinking about Sutton?"

My stomach burns with need at just the mention of his name.

Cara laughs. "You can't hide it, and why should you? Guy's a snack. There's no way around that."

When I turn to her, she throws her hands up in defense. "Relax. I'm not interested. Rest assured I have no interest in hooking up with the alpha, nor him with me."

I hate it, but her calling out my jealousy actually eases it a bit. Sutton *isn't* a snack—he's an entire fucking buffet of bottled-up passion and the promise of an orgasm unlike any other. And if it weren't for the blue-balls-inducing sparks shooting from my fingertips every time things get hot, I would have absolutely already slept with him.

More than once.

"Things are complicated," I say honestly. While I won't full-on admit to this cock-blocking magic I possess, it's the truth. Things go far beyond that with him and me.

We're knee-deep in a murder mystery that might very well end with one or both of us dead.

"Complicated things are almost always the most rewarding," Cara replies as we cross the boundary line into town. It no longer bars entry, nor does it even ripple at our presence—another sign the magic separating Sutton from the others is completely destroyed. I should be happy about that, but instead, I'm left wondering how in the hell it happened in the first place.

"True. But I just got out of a relationship that was headed for the altar, so jumping into another one is probably not a great idea." The excuse is smooth, realistic, and just that—an excuse. Truth is I haven't thought of Roscoe much since I arrived here.

And our breakup feels like it took place in another timeline entirely.

"Oh? I didn't know that."

"Yeah. He was a lawyer who dipped his wick in his paralegal."

"Eww."

"Pretty much."

"I hope you nut-punched him," she says as we step up to a brick building with the words *The Old Fashioned* illuminated in bright yellow.

"The Old Fashioned?"

She grins at me. "Best and only bar in town."

I glance down at our clothes. "We're dressed for a nightclub."

"So? How often does a girl get to dress up these days?"

She doesn't bother waiting for a response before she pulls open the door and ushers me inside. A man with a guitar sits in the corner on a stool, singing an acoustical remix of Coldplay's hit *Yellow*. Patrons sit at the tables, some turned toward him, others wrapped up in their own conversation.

A long bar spans nearly the length of the place, and behind it, a man wearing a white apron serves drinks to the people crowding around.

"This is the most packed I've seen it in a while," Cara observes.

"People need to forget. Alcohol helps with that," I reply.

It doesn't take me long to spot an unfriendly face in the corner, though. George sits in a booth on the far side of the room, already glaring at me. Across from him, I can barely make out two more heads over the top of the high booth seat. They turn to look at me. Then all three men turn back to one another, falling into hushed conversation at their own table.

Fun. A little anti-Serenity and Sutton powwow.

"Mable," Cara exclaims as she crosses the room and slides onto a barstool next to the librarian. I do the same, just on her opposite side.

Mable smiles brightly at me. "You look lovely."

"Thanks. What are you drinking?"

She blushes. "An old fashioned."

"Is it any good?" I ask. "I've never been much of a bourbon drinker."

"Trust me, Ernie will change your mind," she says, not meeting my eyes. "He certainly changed mine."

With a grin, I look up at the bartender and raise my hand. A broad-shouldered man with graying hair and a fully gray mustache rushes over quickly, and Mable's cheeks turn crimson. *Interesting.* "What can I get you?" he asks.

"I'll have one of these," I say, gesturing to Mable's drink.

"Make that two," Cara corrects cheerfully.

He taps a hand on the bar and nods. "You got it, ladies. Mable, you want another?"

"Yes, please, Ernie, thanks."

He beams at her, and my heart warms. "You got it, beautiful."

Mable's crush is obvious and pretty much the most adorable thing I've ever seen. But since the wolves have incredible hearing, I keep my comments to myself. I don't want to embarrass her.

"So, what are you two doing out and about tonight?" Mable questions.

"I figured Serenity needed a girls' night out. Something to blow off some steam."

"I couldn't agree more. Thank you," she adds as Ernie sets three glasses down in front of us.

"Anytime, if you need anything else, let me know." Then, he winks and leaves.

"Oh shit, here comes Jolene," Cara shivers. "Not the friendliest, but I swear she puts crack in her coffee."

I stiffen. While she's been sending coffee out to the house for me, I haven't seen her one-on-one since before the ball, so when she actually approaches the area where I'm sitting, nerves unfurl in my belly.

"Serenity," she greets, sliding onto a stool one over from mine.

"Jolene. Thanks for the coffee you sent over. I appreciate it."

She purses her lips, and the vibe coming off her is as chilly as it's always been. "You're welcome. I didn't expect to see you out."

"Just trying to take a break from it all," I say with forced friendliness.

She glances past me, giving Cara a once-over. Then, she turns her attention to the bar. "Ernie, can I get a whiskey sour? And three shots of Jameson for my friends here."

"You got it." He grabs a glass and begins pouring.

"Shots?" I question, and Jolene side-eyes me.

"Consider it a welcome gift."

I would. Except she doesn't seem very welcoming.

"Thanks," I tell her, "But you don't have to do that—"

"You're right," she says and slaps some bills onto the counter in exchange for the drinks Ernie has set out. Grabbing her whiskey sour, she turns to me as she leaves and adds, "That's what makes it a gift."

I look at Cara, who shrugs.

"Thanks," I say as she walks away.

Ernie picks up the shots. Then, he hands one to Cara, one to me, and one to Mable, who tries to protest.

"Oh yes," Cara says. "Mable, you're doing one, too."

"I don't—"

"You can't argue because you are now officially a part of our girls' night," I tell her.

"Oh, all right." She picks up her shot.

"Here's to being the hottest bitches in the room." Cara winks and turns her glass up. Mable and I share a look before we do the same.

The whiskey burns the back of my throat, but I'm already wanting another. Maybe Cara's on to something with ladies' night. It's been way too long since I let myself chill out and unwind. Mable throws hers back with an expertise I honestly hadn't expected from the quiet librarian.

"Whoo!" Cara shakes her head a little and sets her glass aside. "Okay, Serenity, I now know you have an ex and you were a reporter. What else is there to know about you?" When I raise an eyebrow, she shrugs. "The journalist in me."

Chuckling, I take a drink of my old fashioned.

Mable was right. It's good. "There's really not much else to tell. I have parents, who I'm close to, and four older brothers."

"Wow," Cara says. "That's a lot of testosterone in your house."

I snort. "You have no idea. My oldest brother, Steven, is a homicide detective in New York. I suppose he pushed me to be as curious as I am, though he'd kick my ass sideways if he knew what I was getting into while I'm here." Smiling, I try to ignore the pain in my chest. I miss my family far more than I was prepared to. Mainly because I hadn't planned on being gone this long.

"And the ex?" Cara prompts. "Or if that's too personal, how about the job at the Times?"

"Ugh. Roscoe's not really worth mentioning, though it is connected to my job—or lack thereof."

"Oh, no, what happened?" Mable asks, concern knitting her brow.

"The short version is that I got dumped in public, then proceeded to get hammered, and forgot to turn in a story featuring food truck murder."

"Food truck murder?" Cara's eyes widen. "Seriously?"

"Oh yeah. Burger lady was murdered by the

gumbo guy because both of them were sleeping with the taco truck dude."

Cara snorts and tips her glass up. "That's—wow. And I thought we had drama."

Mable just continues to stare at me wide-eyed.

I snort. Back then it seemed like such a big deal, but now? When compared with a murdering witch who has managed to trap an entire town? It might as well be little more than a blip. "Anyway, I was kind of a mess, trying to figure out my next move when I came home and found newspaper clippings waiting for me in an envelope."

"Newspaper clippings?" Cara questions.

I down the rest of my drink, the alcohol numbing my senses just enough to have me relaxing. Damn, I haven't felt this good since I got here. "Not sure who sent them, but they were local edition articles documenting the unsolved murders. My plan was to come here, solve them, write a story that would knock my boss's socks off, and get my job back."

Both women are silent for a moment. "And instead, you got trapped in a town by two witches, all while trying to ignore your attraction for a certain wolf shifter," Cara comments. "What a lucky girl you are."

Snorting, I nod. Ernie replaces my empty drink without me having to ask, so I tip it up and down a good portion of it. "Yeah, I won the lotto."

"I'm so sorry you're trapped here with us." Mable touches my hand. "Do you regret it?"

I consider her question. "I did at first. But now? I'm starting to believe I'm supposed to be here. My mom always says everything happens for a reason."

Mable smiles. "You've done a lot for us."

"You have," Cara adds. "Breaking part of the curse—or, at least, that's what the rumor is."

I shake my head, noting the way my eyes blur a bit with the movement. A definite buzz has kicked in. "I don't know how I did that or even if it was me. Maybe something went wrong with the spell."

"Maybe," Cara says, though she doesn't look convinced.

Mable frowns. "I doubt it. This has been going on for over a hundred years. For Myrtle to make a mistake now... it doesn't make sense."

We fall into complete silence; a dark, dreary mood overtaking the laughter from minutes ago. It feels wrong, though, to celebrate when this place—these people—have lost so much.

"Wait a damned minute." Cara shoots up from

her chair and points at me. "No. No. No! No more doom and gloom. We promised."

Mable cocks her head to the side. "Promised what?"

"No talk about witches, werewolves, or what-the-fuckery tonight. We are normal women out for a drink and a night of partying." She whirls. "Collin! Karaoke!"

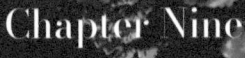

Chapter Nine

The chill in the air feels refreshing against my flushed skin as Cara and I make our way home through the woods. My toe catches on something, and I stumble, nearly face-planting before Cara grabs me and pulls me upright. My heel comes off in the process, wedged into the soft dirt beneath my feet.

"Shit," I hiss, reaching down to scoop up what's left of my shoe. Then, I slip off the other shoe, opting to go barefoot. Seems safer. After two hours of karaoke with bottomless drinks to match, I'm drunker than I've been in a long time—well, aside from my Adele marathon post-breakup. I'm not sure I'll ever top that night, though. Hell, I'm not sure I want to.

Cara urges me onward from where I've halted. "Girl, we need to move our asses before Sutton comes looking and I'm in trouble."

"Hold on," I say then hiccup.

I'm readjusting my grip on my heels when my balance wobbles, and I nearly fall again, thanks to what looks like the same overgrown tree root. Damn thing has it out for me tonight. Cara yanks me up just in time, locking elbows, and we both dissolve into laughter at my clumsiness.

The sound echoes against the silence, but the stillness of the woods doesn't bother me. Not tonight. There's more than enough moonlight to see where I'm going, and I've had more than enough alcohol to fuel my sense of bravery.

In other words, liquid courage.

"You have to walk straight," Cara says as we weave left to right, narrowly avoiding a tree trunk. At least, this time, it belongs to a different tree.

"I am," I say. "You're crooked."

"I'm not crooked."

"Fine, the trees are crooked."

We both crack up again.

"You think Sutton's waiting up for you?" Cara asks.

"Ten bucks says he's standing on the damn porch."

"I'm surprised he hasn't come looking yet, honestly," Cara says with a snort. "The way he watches you... he's like a dog with his bone."

"I'd like to bone *him*," I say, and we both hoot with laughter. I hadn't realized how badly I needed the normalcy of tonight. It's been far too long since I enjoyed hanging out with a friend. Shit, even before I came here, it had been months since Allison and I went out. Roscoe looked down on party girls, and I'd changed myself to fit into his box.

Never again.

From now on, the dude will have to fit into my box. I snicker at the dirty undertone of my own thoughts. And then inevitably picture Sutton trying to fit into my box. Even the mental image is torture right now.

"Speaking of boning," Cara says, pulling me from my fantasies, "am I the only one who noticed the tension between Mable and Ernie back there?"

"Nope," I say, popping the "p" extra hard. "Those two are adorable. But how long do you think Mable's been harboring a crush? I mean, haven't they known each other for like a century now? It seems a little ridiculous at this point—like, just go for it already."

"I think we've all been living in a sort of holding pattern," she says with a shrug. "I mean, we've been trapped here for a hundred years. Our lives are sort of frozen. Until that changes, what's the point of anything else, you know?"

Her words penetrate my drunken state, reminding me once again what all these people have lost. And more, what they stand to gain if I can help them. It's sobering as hell.

"What about you?" She bumps my hip, which sends us veering left. "What's keeping you and Sutton from doing the dirty—"

A *crack* sounds from nearby, and I picture a branch snapping.

We both shut up and stare at each other wide-eyed.

"What was that?" I whisper.

Although, I'm pretty sure it comes out way too loud.

"Someone's out here," Cara says, looking worried.

Shit. If she's worried, I'm definitely worried. After all, she can go all wolf girl, and I'm just a measly human who supposedly has witch powers she can't actually use.

"Who?" I ask.

She shakes her head to indicate she doesn't know. "Don't move."

My ears strain to hear anything else, and all I can think is, if a bear shows up, I'm not sure Cara's current state will allow her to fight it off like Sutton once did. And I damn sure won't be fighting anything except gravity and a loose bladder in my current state either.

Snap.

Another branch. This time, it's closer.

If I strain, I can hear footsteps as they crunch over the dried brush covering the ground.

Cara tries to move but wobbles when her heel sticks in the ground.

Suddenly, having a drunken Cara as my escort home through the woods at midnight doesn't seem like the smartest plan. *Sutton is going to kill me. Unless whoever's out there does it first.*

Cara holds a finger to her lips, and I nod.

The footsteps are nearly upon us. Don't have to tell me twice.

Cara drags me behind a tree, which, even buzzed, I

know is stupid since the trunk is only wide enough to cover maybe a hipbone each. We're completely exposed with nowhere to go. And I'm not dumb enough to think I can outrun a damn thing in this town. Even sober, I'd be nothing but prey to these people.

Illuminated by moonlight, a figure walks into view, and I gasp.

Yvette.

Her head whips toward me, and our eyes lock.

"Hello, Serenity." Her voice is scratchy as if she hasn't used it in a while. But otherwise, she looks fine. Freshly showered, clean clothes, combed hair. My eyes narrow as I try to figure out how she's here, looking like she hasn't been in hiding while we've hunted her nonstop for days.

"What do you want?" Cara asks.

She sounds just as shocked as I am to see the witch.

Yvette cocks her head at Cara. There's a moment of hesitation as she looks between Cara and me. In that split second, I can feel energy rising inside me, and I hold my breath as my fingertips zing with blue magic.

Yes.

If I can just—

"I came for her," Yvette says, nodding at me. "You're going to pay for the damage you've done."

"Damage?" I repeat. "Are you serious?"

"You've destroyed the hard work my sister has put in to avenge my niece." She raises her hands, and her expression twists into an angry snarl. "And now you'll pay."

Magic slams into me with the force of a train.

I'm thrown backward, knocked on my ass hard enough that I can barely pry my eyes open as I struggle to get up. Pain shoots up my back and then lances through my left arm when I roll to the side, my stomach rolling along with it.

"Serenity, run!" Cara screams.

But I can't even walk. Not with my head still spinning.

I prop myself on my elbow and look up in time to see Cara limping away. She doesn't get far before a blast of magic hits her squarely between the shoulders. She grunts and falls face-first into the dirt.

She doesn't get up again.

I'm too shocked to even scream. Cara, a werewolf with strength far beyond mine, is down. And I have no doubt I'll be next. Is this how I'm going to go out? Drunk in the woods and shot dead by a witch's magic bullets? Are you fucking kidding me?

Yvette turns back to me, stalking closer to where I'm still struggling to get on my feet again. Fear grips me as reality sinks in. I'm alone out here with a very angry, very powerful witch, who thinks I fucked with her sister and deserve to be punished for it. A sibling bent on protection is a dangerous thing even without magic involved—I would know.

"You don't have to do this, Yvette." I inch backward, for all the good that does. "You can still walk away. Have a life of your own."

"You ruined what my sister worked so hard to create," she says, striding toward me. "I must avenge that, or else what kind of sister would I be?"

She doesn't give me a chance to answer before she blasts me again. I roll sideways, taking the brunt of the hit against my hip. The fabric of my dress singes with the heat of its impact. My skin burns, and I grimace as I scramble to my feet.

Yvette stands before me, her twisted smile making it clear she's enjoying this little game. I have no doubt she could end this anytime, but she's toying with me. It pisses me off, and that anger has me running my mouth—the only weapon I have left.

"Your sister is a psychotic bitch," I tell her. "Wrecking lives all because her own daughter was apparently a chip off the old block. Looks like crazy runs in your entire family."

Yvette's eyes narrow.

Okay, maybe talking shit to the murdering old lady wasn't the smartest thing to do.

"You're going to regret your insults." Yvette raises her hand, and I brace myself, knowing full well this will be the killing strike—but it never comes.

On my right, a snarl sounds. Angry, rageful—and all too familiar.

Sutton's wolf emerges out of the darkness. He springs forward and launches himself at Yvette. Hope blooms inside my aching chest. We're safe. He'd never let anything happen to me.

He's come like I knew he would.

Yvette throws her hand up toward Sutton, and magic slices through him. He falls out of the air, a pained yelp escaping as he lands in the dirt several yards short of the woman he intended to attack.

I feel it like a punch in the gut.

Yvette turns slowly back to me, a batshit crazy self-satisfied smile on her lips.

This. Bitch.

"Now," she says, "Where were we?"

"You did not just attack my man." My energy spikes, my hardened voice unfamiliar to me as I climb to my feet.

Yvette does nothing. And why would she? She thinks she's already won, so why not let me stand up first? Ugh. Fear, anguish, desperation—it crashes together, and I don't think. I just act.

My hands shove at the air between us, and magic flies from my fingers. Blue sparks that grow stronger and hotter until it's a wall of flame aimed straight for Yvette. She screams as the magic hits her, and I watch as she goes down in a crumpled heap. Her clothes smoke, and her skin burns as the fire consumes her. The stench of charred skin fills my nose, but I'm far too angry to puke.

This bitch hurt Sutton. She's going to die for it.

Screams split the air, and she thrashes on the ground, rolling to try and put out the consuming blue fire. The gut-wrenching sound of her pain both disgusts and satisfies me until the moment her screams cease. The woods around us fall eerily silent.

I drop my hands and rush to Sutton. Resting a hand on his furry neck, I lean down. "Sutton?"

His eyes are closed. I can't even tell if he's

breathing. Dread coils in my stomach, and tears burn the back of my throat. I run my palms along his fur, urging him to wake up. Something warm coats my fingers, and I pull them back. Beneath the light of the moon, I can see the dark crimson blood staining my skin.

Tremors take over my body. "Sutton!"

No answer.

A sob builds in my throat.

Fear threatens to tear me apart. More magic leaks from my hands, but I ignore it, gripping him tighter. It's an easy draw now, the power inside me. Whatever I just did to Yvette somehow broke whatever barrier had been keeping it from me. Now, I can barely stop it from flowing at all. None of it affects Sutton, though. Not like it did before. And that, more than anything, scares me.

Is it because he's—

"Sutton, wake the fuck up right now," I demand.

In the distance, a wolf howls.

Someone knows we're here. The pack will probably arrive soon enough.

My eyes blur with tears because, in this moment, there isn't a damn thing anyone else can do. The damage has already been done. It's too late.

"Sutton, I mean it. If you die, I will kill you," I

threaten, barely holding back a sob. My fingers tighten on his fur.

A faint grumble sounds from his wolf's chest, and I straighten, afraid to hope. The noise comes again, and Sutton stirs. I concentrate on pulling my magic back. The last thing I want to do is injure him further.

His form trembles, and his massive claws twitch dangerously close to my exposed skin. I jump clear just as he shifts back to his human form and opens his eyes.

He looks up at me, blood coating most of his skin; a dark crimson so thick I can't even make out where it's coming from.

"You're alive," I say, choking on my relief.

He reaches for me, tensing with what I can only imagine is pain. I grab his hand, sinking down beside him once more. A single shard of magic sparks between us and then fades. I try to pull my hand away, but he holds tight.

"You're not going to get away from me that easily," he says, voice rough and strained.

Maybe it's the alcohol still flowing in my veins. Or the fact that I'm pretty sure I just killed a woman. But his words pull a dark and heady laugh from me. And once I start, I can't stop. It's something out of a Disney villain moment. My head tipped back, my tangled hair flowing down my back, the unhinged sound of my own laughter ringing in my ears. I cackle until tears run down my cheeks and my ribs ache from the effort.

Sutton looks at me like I've lost it. Maybe I have.

"What's so funny?" he asks when I finally quiet enough for him to get a word in.

"Oh, nothing," I tell him. "Just that I killed an old lady and figured out I'm in love with a werewolf all in the same night. And the only thing I'll probably regret tomorrow is the karaoke."

Chapter Ten

"Thank you, Jasper," Sutton says to the tall dark-haired man currently standing on the porch.

Soft moonlight frames both their faces, but over Jasper's shoulder, I can see where late-night shadows creep toward the house from the dark woods beyond. With a shudder, I turn away, reminding myself we're both alive and well—and Yvette is neither.

"No problem, alpha," Jasper says. "I'll have a guard posted outside for the rest of the night. And we'll see to it that Cara gets home safe."

"Great. I'll check in with you tomorrow." Sutton closes the door, making it just the two of us in the house for the first time since I left hours ago for a night out that turned into a freaking night*mare*.

Jasper was the first to show and the last to leave, which makes him my current favorite pack member as far as I'm concerned. But now that I'm home, I don't know what to do next. From where I stand near the stairs, I have a front-row seat to Sutton's blood-smeared back, and I can't make myself look away.

Tears blur my vision, the effects of the adrenaline and alcohol both gone, leaving me to deal with the events of what happened tonight completely sober. I almost lost him. And the thing that guts me most about that moment is that I never really had him to begin with.

He turns, and my gaze drops to the huge wound on his side. Thanks to his abilities, it's already started healing, but the center is raw, bloody, and looks like it hurts like hell. "First-aid kit?" I manage, my voice hoarse. The need to do something—anything to soothe his pain is overwhelming.

Brows drawn together, he nods toward the hall on the right. "Bathroom."

Leaving him standing in the entryway, I all but sprint to the bathroom. It was my fault he had to come after me tonight in the first place. If I'd have stayed sober, or, at the very least, insisted on a group versus one intoxicated she-wolf to walk me home, he likely wouldn't have been injured. And Cara wouldn't have been knocked unconscious or woken with a possible concussion.

In the bathroom, I fling open the cabinet and scan the contents inside. It doesn't take me but a few seconds to find the small red case, so I find my way back to Sutton as he's lowering himself on a stool in the kitchen. I drop to my knees and open the lid on the medical kit.

"You don't need to do that."

"Shut up," I snap. "Unless you want it to get infected." I tear open an alcohol swab and gently touch it to his side.

He hisses. "Shit. I think you made it worse."

I glare up at him.

Sutton smiles softly. "Serenity, it's okay."

"No. It's not." I sniffle, and he slips out of the stool to kneel beside me.

"I will be healed by the time you can finish cleaning it." He cups my cheeks and runs his thumbs over my skin. Then, he tilts my head to the side and narrows his gaze. "You, on the other hand…"

Grabbing some gauze and a small brown bottle, he brushes the hair off of my neck. I tilt my head to the side to give him access. Cold moisture hits an open wound I didn't even know I had, and I grind my teeth together against the sting.

"Sorry." He gently wipes it then pulls back, showing me the white gauze crusted with blood. After setting the gauze and bottle onto the floor, he takes my hands. "It's not too bad."

My throat constricts. "I'm so sorry I screwed up."

"How did you screw up?"

"I was drunk. Walking in the woods. Take your pick."

Sutton's mouth quirks. "Seems to me you're beating yourself up just fine for the both of us." Standing, he pulls me to my feet. "Now, I don't know about you, but I'd love a shower."

He hasn't mentioned my confession yet, or the fact that I killed a woman tonight, and I can't decide whether I'm relieved or pissed off at the elephant in the room. He wraps an arm around my waist and guides me toward the stairs.

"Why haven't you said anything?" I demand, settling on feeling pissed off.

Tell a guy you love him and he acts like nothing

has changed. An especially frustrating response given he's been more than open about how he feels about me.

He doesn't try to deny or sidestep the topic of conversation. Instead, he releases me so I can face him. "I didn't feel like bringing up something that might have just been effects of the alcohol or adrenaline."

"It wasn't." The air around us shifts, and my heart begins to pound. "I meant what I said. Almost losing you—I can't lose you, Sutton."

"I'm not looking to play games, Serenity."

"Neither am I." To demonstrate, I take a step closer. His nostrils flare, his pupils dilating as he looks down at me. With a trembling hand, I reach forward and touch his blood-smeared chest. The muscles beneath my palm are warm, inviting, so I add my other hand.

Sutton's eyes close, and he breathes deeply. I know he senses my lust, and somehow, it only makes the moment even hotter.

Tired of waiting, I stretch up and gently press my lips to his. A tender kiss to test the waters. And, thankfully, lacking one cock-blocking blue spark. The moment Sutton realizes my spark isn't going to stop us, he reacts.

Sutton's hand grips the back of my neck, and he spins me, pressing my back to the wall behind me as he takes my mouth. Gone is the sensual savoring from a moment ago. Sutton is an animal, and I've just set him free. His hands tangle in my hair as his tongue traces the seam of my lips. His roughness triggers something in me, and my grief vanishes. In its place is a desperation that threatens to snap my own careful control. I don't want gentle right now. I want Sutton Hargrave.

I open beneath him, and he fucking consumes me.

Hands slipping down my body, he grips my ass and lifts me, his hard length pressing right against my center as he pins me to the wall.

I don't care that we're covered in dirt and grime. Don't care that tonight nearly went horribly wrong. Because right now, it's just me and him. And I want him. Desperately. Against the wall, on the stairs, the bed—I don't care.

Holding me tightly against his body, he ascends the stairs one by one, still fucking my mouth with a tongue that I *know* can work magic.

If he tries to stop now, I'll kill him myself.

Somehow, we make it into the bathroom, and he manages to turn the water on. It slaps the tile and

Sutton pins me against the wall again, a low growl escaping his lips as he trails his tongue over my jaw, my neck.

Every nerve in my body is ablaze, every fiber of my being consumed by the man before me.

His fingers sear my skin as he carries me into the shower, me still fully clothed. Lukewarm water hits my back, but it doesn't cool the fire between us. Like gasoline on a flame, it ignites.

My hands grip the thick strands of his hair. He sets me on my feet and grabs my dress, ripping it open. I gasp as he throws the tattered remnants of my dress to the tile at our feet. His hand palms my breast, thumb and finger gently pinching the peak of my nipple.

Warmth burns me up from the inside, and I arch back.

"You drive me mad," he growls in my ear before nipping my jaw.

There has to be something wrong with me because it turns me on like nothing else, and I want him to bite me again.

Grabbing the waistband of his shorts, I shove them down, exposing every inch of his naked body.

My mouth goes dry.

My heart pumps.

Sutton is fucking *huge*. And why wouldn't he be? Everything about this man is larger than life. He cups the back of my neck and yanks me to him. I grip his length, squeezing gently. He thrusts into my hand, and I squeeze it harder, sliding my hand over his hard length.

He spins me, pressing my front to the shower. His hard body at my back, I'm pinned. Trapped. And so fucking turned on I can barely breathe.

Sutton's free hand goes to my hip, and he squeezes, sliding down over my ass and between my thighs. He brushes his fingers over me, and I gasp.

"You are so perfect," he whispers in my ear. "I don't know where I should touch you. It feels like we've waited so long."

"I want you," I choke out. "Please."

Sutton chuckles, the sound an aphrodisiac. I slide my legs apart a little more. He cups me from behind, his hand so close to my ass I don't know whether to be nervous or exhilarated. "What should I do with you now that I have you?"

Here, at the mercy of an alpha, I've never felt so powerful. My body jerks when he slides a finger over my clit. Every muscle in my body tightens, preparing for what is promising to be the release to end all releases. "Sutton," I moan, his name a plea. "Please."

"Please, what?" he growls, his finger moving torturously slow over me. Every touch sets my blood afire.

"Let me—" I arch back, my head falling against his chest.

"Not until you ask," he growls. "What do you want from me?"

"Please," I pant. "Faster. Let me come."

He picks up the pace, sliding one finger inside of me. Then two. He fucks me with his fingers as his thumb caresses my clit. Stars explode in my vision, and I cry out, my hands grasping for the tile even as it offers no support.

My legs go weak.

He continues sliding his fingers in and out, in and out, slowing down each time to draw out all of my pleasure until I'm completely mindless.

Then, he withdraws his fingers and turns me to face him. Hair soaking wet, the water drips down over his body, each droplet caressing muscles I want to touch. Taste.

I want everything. All he has.

Sutton steps closer and lifts me again. I wrap both legs around his waist, kissing him with feverish passion. Cold air nips at my skin as he carries me out of the shower. He crosses the room and throws me back onto his bed, completely soaked.

His massive hands go to my knees, and he spreads my legs, chewing on his bottom lip as he stares at me. I'm fully exposed, completely open to him, and he looks hungrily at what I'm offering.

"You are so fucking delicious," he growls as he climbs onto the bed between my legs. Leaning forward, he aligns with my body, pressing his length against my entrance.

"Please," I choke out.

"I already told you my rule, Serenity. Tell me what you want."

"You," I whisper.

Sutton beams at me. With one thrust, he buries himself in me, and I cry out.

Sutton groans and stills. "You're so fucking tight."

"You're so fucking large," I shoot back.

He pulls back and drives into me again. Again. Again. Each thrust pushes me closer and closer toward the edge. "I want to see you," he growls and rolls over, taking me with him so I'm on top. My palms splay over his muscled chest, and he reaches up to cup my breasts.

I move, driving us at the speed of my own heart until—throwing my head back, I scream his name, the orgasm tearing me apart into a million tiny pieces. He flips me back over and drives into me faster, a furious, punishing pace, until he pulls out and rolls over to his back.

He strokes himself once before his own release takes over. Seconds tick by, each of us still reeling from what had to be an award-winning bang.

"That was—" I start, breathless.

"Worth nearly dying for?" he questions.

Cracking an eye open I glare at him. "You tell me."

Sutton chuckles and gets to his feet. "What I will tell you is that I am nowhere near done with you, Serenity Kellis." Gripping my hand, he yanks me up and pulls me toward the bathroom for round two.

"Is that a threat or a promise?" I joke.

But the gleam in his eye holds no humor as he tells me, "Both."

Chapter Eleven

I wake to the feel of a hand trailing over my bare shoulder and up my collarbone. A zing of pleasure trails with it. I inhale deeply. The scent of sex and Sutton Hargrave reminds me exactly where I am—and what I've done. My eyes open, and I smile at the sight of Sutton's face staring back at me. His chin bears a layer of stubble I remember scratching along my thighs last night. And his long hair hangs in his eyes but not so much that I can't see the desire reflected in their depths. He's propped on his elbow and watching me with a look of reverence that touches parts of me I'm surprised to find haven't felt this way... ever.

"Good morning," I say sleepily.

"Mm, morning." He leans down and presses a

kiss to my lips that's probably supposed to be chaste and quick, but one taste of him, and my body takes over. Lips still locked, I reach up and wrap my arms around his neck, pulling him down over me and reveling in the feel of his weight against me.

"I didn't mean to wake you," he says between kisses.

"Yeah, that was a real dick move," I murmur.

He grins down at me. "Pun intended?"

"Ugh," I groan. "My point is you can make it up to me with an orgasm."

"Are you sure you're up for that? I could have sworn the last thing you said before you fell asleep was 'if I can't walk tomorrow, it's your fault.'"

I wiggle my legs out from under him, stretching and bending them for effect. "I'm not saying you didn't do your job, but..."

I yelp as he tickles me, both of us laughing while we sexy-wrestle our way toward round six... or seven. I've lost count. All I know is every single round has been toe-curling and delicious, and I really might walk with a limp when I finally get out of this bed again. His bed. Or ours. It's getting a bit hard to know for sure.

A problem that seems delightful compared to

the true reality that awaits me when I come down from my sex high.

Am I using Sutton's body as a distraction from the horrors that await us when we're done? Damn right I am. Do I think he minds? Abso-freaking-lutely not.

The tickling turns to stroking. My laughter turns to heavy sighs as Sutton's hands grip my arms and yank them over my head, pinning them to the mattress. He trails his nose over my throat and inhales. "What to do with you," he whispers.

I arch up into him, pressing my center to him, and he groans. "I can think of a few ideas," I reply.

Sutton chuckles and releases my hands, pulling back until he's kneeling at my side. "So can I." Reaching forward, he flips me over so my stomach is pressed to the mattress. The covers completely leave my body, and his fingertips go to my spine.

A soft moan leaves my lips as he trails his fingers down my back. When he shifts his weight and nudges my legs open with his knee, a small bite of fear shoots through me.

On my belly, I feel more exposed than ever. Especially when he cups my ass with both hands and then slides one down to the part of me that aches for him. I moan, arching my back to give him more access.

Sutton's hot breath fans over my thighs, and I still. He chuckles. "Am I making you nervous?"

"A little," I admit. This happens to be the closest any man has ever been to my ass, and, well, given his size, I can't say I'm jumping at the idea of expanding our sexual adventure.

"I'm not after that, Serenity. At least, not yet," he whispers as the hand cupping me grips my thigh, folding my leg up to give him better access. He runs his tongue over me, and I cry out, pleasure rocketing through my core. One hand pins my thigh to the side. The other slips between my body and the mattress to caress my clit as he slides his tongue into me.

"Sutton!" I cry out, my hands fisting the sheets as he continues driving me closer and closer to the edge.

Release shatters me, and Sutton moves quickly, sliding up my body and driving into me from behind. He grips my hips, each thrust drawing out every bit of pleasure from my body. We clash together, two pieces that fit perfectly together until—

"Fuck," Sutton growls and pulls out, rolling

onto his back and pumping himself with his hand until his own release breaks free.

Together, we suck in deep breaths, one after the other, my heart hammering. I honestly cannot even put into words how amazing that was. And yet, I honestly believe I've only just scratched the surface of the pleasure this man can bring me.

"Shit." Sutton jumps out of bed and heads for the bathroom. I sit up against the bed, waiting for him.

"What is it?"

He steps out of the bathroom wearing sweats as someone pounds on the door. "You'd better cover up."

Panic claws at my throat as I imagine Myrtle here to rain down vengeance for what I've done to her sister.

I killed Yvette.

The events of last night come crashing down around me, and my mind fills with the horrific image of Sutton covered in blood, unmoving.

"It's okay," Sutton says, probably in response to the rapid thudding of my heart. "It's just Jasper. But if he sees you naked, I will have to kill him."

I cover up quickly, and Sutton pulls open the

door, though I cannot make out what is spoken between the two.

He turns toward me. "Meet us downstairs," he says, wearing a grim expression on his face, then slips out and shuts the door behind him.

I scramble to catch up, grabbing whatever clothes I can find on my way to the door.

Turns out, I *can* walk and dress, but running while pulling on leggings is a bit harder. I nearly trip down the stairs as I struggle to get down them while pulling the leggings into place over my bare ass. At the bottom of the steps, I land hard and look up at both Sutton and Jasper watching me from the foyer.

Jasper's expression is grim, and Sutton doesn't look any better. The fact that Sutton doesn't tease me about my legs not working means something's up.

"What happened?" I ask, adjusting my shirt to make sure everything's covered.

"Harriet Patmore was found dead this morning," Sutton says.

Harriet? "The woman who sent us the basket of tea?"

Her gift had been among the others, along with a very kind note that didn't pressure me to do anything other than to "take care in these hard times."

"Yes," Sutton says.

A slow dread works its way through me. "How did she die?"

I pretend he's going to say heart attack, accident, old age—anything but what he says next. "Her throat was cut open and drained of blood. Near the old ward lines at the edge of town."

"Wait. You mean the boundary that separated the woods from the town? The one you couldn't cross before...?"

His non-answer is all I need to know. My stomach plummets.

Myrtle.

"She's trying to restart that part of the spell," I say.

Sutton and Jasper exchange a look.

"What?" I demand.

"My father tried coming to the house earlier," Sutton says. "He couldn't get through."

"Wards won't let him pass," Jasper adds.

"It's working," I realize. "Whatever she's doing with Harriet's blood, it's working." I look at Sutton, fear making it hard to breathe. "She's trying to cut you off from everyone again." The look in his eye is pure misery, and I realize how badly this will set him back if Myrtle succeeds in trapping him again.

"She knows we're stronger as a pack," Jasper says.

He sounds angry, ready to fight—but how can we do that when the enemy won't face us?

Yvette faced us out of anger—and lost. But Yvette is not Myrtle. Myrtle has proven to be calculated and incredibly patient.

I ball my hands into fists, feeling the magic surge inside me. I have no idea what made it stay hidden last night while Sutton and I... But it's back now, and I can't afford to hurt anyone else. Not until Myrtle is the one standing before me.

"We need to go into town," I say. "So she can't lock you out."

"And then what?" Sutton asks. "We'll be exposed. And that's what she wants ultimately." His expression hardens. "I won't put you in danger, Serenity."

"You can stay with me," Jasper says, but Sutton shakes his head.

"I won't put you in danger either. It's me she wants."

I bite my lip. "We'll figure it out. But we should get moving, or we won't be able to get out at all."

They both agree, and after a quick grab of the things I need, we meet back at the front door. It's a sad collection of items that I'm carrying. Most of them don't belong to me. Not really. A pair of jeans and a jacket Cara sent over. A few toiletries gifted to me by the pack. I bring the tea—mostly because it feels disrespectful to Harriet's memory to leave it behind.

I'm ready faster than Sutton and end up outside with Jasper while we wait.

He's quiet, though I get the feeling that's just his nature.

"You okay?" he asks finally.

"I mean, Yvette's no longer a threat, so that's … a relief. But—"

"Taking a life isn't for the faint of heart," he finishes. Then his mouth tips up in a haunted smile. "You're not faint of heart, though, Serenity Kellis."

Before I can ask how he knows that, Sutton returns. At the same time he steps outside, Cara appears from the trail, breathless.

I drop everything I'm carrying and throw my arms around her neck.

"Whoa," she says, catching me before I can take us both down.

"You're okay," I say, squeezing until she pries me off her.

"I'm okay," she confirms.

"You were unconscious," I begin. "And they said something about a concussion—"

"Already healed. Wolf power, remember?"

I exhale.

"Look, I'm sorry," she says, hanging her head. "I should have protected you—"

"Are you kidding? You nearly died trying to save me."

"Yeah, but I was stupid. Too many drinks. Not paying attention."

"Neither was I," I tell her. "Consider us even. I'm just glad you're all right."

She grins. "Yeah, thanks to you." She hip-bumps me. "Badass witch slayer."

"We need to get going," Sutton says. "Any trouble?" he asks Cara.

"Woods are clear," she tells him then hangs her head. "And... I'm sorry about last night."

"No need to apologize, I'm just glad you're okay." Though the way he says it is strained. Surely he's not actually mad?

"Thank you," she says, obviously relieved.

"Let's get moving." He takes my hand, and we set off through the trees.

No one says much on the walk toward town. I sense Sutton's thoughts have gone to a dark place, but mine aren't any better. So, I leave it alone.

All too soon, we've reached the outskirts of town. Up ahead, I can see a few pack members guarding an area they've marked off. And in the center, a figure lies prone in the patchy grass.

Harriet.

I slow my pace.

"You don't have to see this," Sutton says.

"Yeah," I say, taking a deep breath. "I think I do."

Harriet's body has been cut and drained—just like the Sheriff's. Just like all the others before.

Judging from the expressions everyone wears, it's a devastating blow. More so than the past victims. Because this time, Myrtle didn't wait until All Hallows Eve to renew the curse's magic. She's thrown out the rules. Making them up as she goes. And that's scarier than anything that's happened yet.

Predictability is what we relied on. If she's not acting as we expect, well, there's no way to know what's coming next. No way to prepare.

Which means Myrtle has all the power—and

despite everything, we still have none. Even with Yvette gone, we have no way to stop this. No way to be free.

I hang back, waiting while Sutton talks to the pack members. I can hear them offering him a place to stay—offering us both. But he turns them all down. I don't blame him. He's protecting them in what little way he can. But we can't be homeless.

When it's clear they're wrapping up, Phineas arrives and embraces Sutton tightly. I can see the worry in both their eyes. They're terrified of being separated again. My heart aches for them. For all of them.

And that ache fuels my determination like never before.

By the time Sutton is finished, most of the others have cleared out.

"Everything okay?" I ask when he approaches me. "They all cleared out so fast."

"My father wanted to get Harriet to the coroner as soon as possible," he explains. "They were friends for a very long time."

"I see." My eyes fill with tears that I refuse to let fall. "Now what?"

He glances back toward the trees. "I've sent a couple of teams to run the perimeter. If Myrtle's out there, casting this spell again, she'll have to do it along the ward lines. If not here then farther out."

"Have they found anything?" I ask.

Before he can answer, a boom sounds. It's not very loud, but when I look up, I see a thin curl of smoke rising in the distance. Unease burns in my gut as my adrenaline spikes.

"Is that—"

"Yes." Sutton's answer is no more than a growl. He starts for the woods in the direction of the smoke, and I grab his arm, stopping him.

"What are you doing?" I demand.

"She can't get away. Not again."

He tries pulling away, which isn't hard because, holy hell, this man is strong. I have zero chance of stopping him if he's decided to go, and fear threatens to rip me apart at what might happen to him if he faces Myrtle alone.

"Sutton, wait," I call, but there's no need.

He makes it all of three steps before he smacks into an invisible barrier and stumbles back again. He straightens, staring at the spot where he was just driven backward. Slower this time, he approaches it again and lifts his hand, palm out. He presses against something, gritting his teeth with the powerful effort he puts behind the motion.

Whatever it is he's trying to move, it doesn't budge.

I step up beside him and press my own hands to what feels like a cold, smooth surface.

Then I yank them back again and stare at Sutton.

"She did it," I say. "She reconstructed the barrier. We're locked out."

Sutton looks torn between relief and misery as he says, "Or locked in."

Chapter Twelve

"Three large coffees, please. Black. Strong." My voice hardly wavers as I place my order.

From across the counter, Jolene nods at me, her typically stony expression softer than usual. With bloodshot eyes, she begins working on the coffees. *Bean There* is all but empty with only two patrons other than myself inside. Since word of Harriet's murder spread, most folks have retreated into their own houses or businesses. Even in broad daylight, the town looks nearly empty. I'm still surprised Sutton let me out of his sight long enough for me to get us coffee. He and Phineas went ahead to the morgue—an errand I decided to opt out of. Mainly because I've hit my quota of dead bodies in the last twenty-four hours. Two is enough and I don't need to see or stand around with any more than that.

"I hear Sutton can't return to his house," a woman whispers loudly in the corner to the man at her table.

"What if we don't have a year? What if this is the year that witch decides to end us all?"

My throat constricts, burning with emotion as I turn to face them. "You cannot give up hope," I tell them.

They simply stare back at me.

"I'm sorry. I didn't mean to eavesdrop." Turning back to the counter, I offer Jolene a twenty, but she shakes her head and hands me the drink carrier.

"Don't worry about it."

"Jolene—"

"Just stop this bitch." Her bottom lip quivers slightly, and the display of emotion is so unlike her I don't even know how to respond. Which is probably a good thing since she immediately turns around and starts letting steam out of a machine.

Drinks in hand, I step out into the dreary afternoon and head down the block toward the police station, which also happens to double as the city morgue. Nothing like a dual-purpose building, I suppose. It's close enough to the coffee shop that

Sutton claimed he'd hear my screams if Myrtle tried anything while I was gone. It took everything in me not to make a crude joke about him enjoying my screams last night, but given the serious nature of what we're dealing with, humor doesn't feel appropriate. At least, not at the moment.

As I walk, I keep my head down, not meeting the eyes of the few people out and about. How can I? I have nothing to say to them. *So sorry I was having the best sex of my life while one of the beloved residents of this town was brutally murdered. Likely because I committed a murder of my own last night. Before said sex, of course.*

A tear slips free, and I angrily wipe it away with my empty hand. Yvette would have killed Sutton. She would have killed me and Cara, too. I will *not* feel guilty about what I did. Not until the rest of this threat has been dealt with. Then there will be plenty of time to focus on crimes committed during my time here.

My phone vibrates in my pocket, the *Bad Boys, Bad Boys, What You Gonna Do?* ringtone signaling just who's on the other end. *Perfect. Just what I need. An interrogation.* "Hello?" I ask, still walking down the street. With both hands occupied—something Steven would chastise me for.

"How's your vacation going?" Steven's tone makes it clear he's so far past believing this is a vacation anymore.

Forcing my fakest voice ever, I reply, "Peachy."

"Peachy, huh? Eating a lot of fruit?"

"Definitely. Peaches, apples, grapes. Virginia is known for its pawpaws."

"What the fuck is a pawpaw?"

"Part of the custard apple family. Delicious." I committed murder yesterday, and now I'm talking to my homicide detective older brother about fruit. What the hell has become of my life?

Steven is silent for a moment. Then I hear him mutter something before returning to the line. "Sorry, working a case where a wife killed her husband and his mistress after engaging in a three-way with them."

"Yikes."

"Understatement. Maybe I'll just take an extended leave of absence and travel to a remote Virginia town, too."

"No." The word comes out faster and harsher than I meant, and knowing Steven, he has now massively read into the response.

"What's going on with you?"

"Nothing is going on. I'm just tired. Lots of hiking."

"Ser—"

"I'm fine, Steven. I promise." Stopping just outside the door to the station, I set the coffees down on a bench and take a seat next to them. "I met someone," I say, hoping like hell it doesn't bite me in the ass.

"And that's fifty bucks for me."

"What the hell does that mean?"

"I bet Dad you'd met someone, which is why you haven't come home."

"You *bet* on me hooking up?"

"And won. That's the important part."

"Are you fucking kidding me, Steven?" For some crazy-ass reason, tears fill my eyes. I can't be mad at him, I know that. It's not like he can ever know I'm over here dealing with life-or-death situations, but shit. I'm facing off with murderous bitches and he's gambling on my sex life. I don't know if I've ever felt so alone as I do right now.

My entire life, I've had my family. I've always been able to be open with them. To ask for help when I need it. And now—now doing so would mean I would lose them, too.

"Why the hell are you so pissy? It's not like my bet was off."

"I'm not mad. I'm sorry." Pinching the bridge of my nose, I will the anger away. "It's just early, and we're still figuring things out."

"What's his name?"

"Nope."

"Serenity Kellis."

"Steven Kellis."

"Give me his name."

"Not yet. When I figure things out, I will."

"Social security number?"

"Nice try."

"I can't exactly run a background check on him without some details."

I snort. "Because a background check let me know Roscoe was going to be a cheating son of a bitch? I'd really rather keep this one quiet for now. Please? Can you just trust me?"

Steven sighs. "Fine. One week. Then I want a name."

I grimace. A week isn't exactly my preferred timeline for dealing with all my problems, but I can't afford to argue either. "Deal."

"Serenity!"

I turn, surprised to see a red-faced Mable rushing toward me.

"I have to go, love you."

"Love you, too."

I shove my phone into my pocket and fully turn to face her just as she comes to a stop. Holding up a finger, she takes a few deep breaths, and I watch, half-amused even as my mood remains somber.

"I thought you were an agile wolf?"

"An out-of-shape one," she jokes. "It's been a while since I had to run." Straightening, her gaze meets mine. "How are you?"

"Not great," I admit. "We have another dead woman, and there was the whole murdering Yvette thing last night. I guess I'm trying to come to terms with condemning Audrey as a murderer and becoming one myself."

"You saved Sutton, Cara, and yourself from Yvette's wrath, you know. That's something to be proud of."

"Maybe."

"There's no maybe about it, Serenity. If it weren't for you and your abilities, we would all still be trapped in our human forms, and the three of you would likely be dead."

"Well, I appreciate your faith in me." I force a smile.

Mable hesitates and begins to fidget with the bottom of her sweatshirt.

"What is it?" I ask. I swear if it's another dead person—

"I have something I need to admit." Her chaste response makes me uneasy.

"What?"

Mable swallows hard and meets my eyes. Every muscle in my body tenses, prepared for her to admit that she's actually Myrtle. Maybe she has been since the night of the ball. Fighting the urge to retreat, I hold my ground.

We're out in the open. Surely—

"I sent you the newspaper clippings," she blurts.

I gape at her. "You sent them to me?"

She nods. "I hired a messenger to deliver them."

"But...why? I mean, why me?"

"When Sutton told me he found the curse breaker, and he told me your name, I looked you up. After that, I followed your work for a long time, and it was so easy to see what a kind, good person you are."

"Wait a damn minute. You sent me those clippings? Are you the one who slipped them under my door at the B&B when I first arrived too?"

She nods again. "After I found out you were the curse breaker, I did research. I looked into you, your family—you are such a good person, Serenity." Reaching forward, she places her hand on my arm. "They believe you are the curse breaker because a witch cast a spell that gave your name. But *I* believe you are the one who will save us because of how strong you are. Because of the depth of your caring and kindness. Because of your heart."

Her words are a comfort, but just as quickly as they soothe me, I'm wary again. "You lied to me. From the moment I stepped into the library."

Mable's hand falls, her expression morphing to one of guilt. "I couldn't tell you. Not until I knew for sure you would stay. I tried, I gave you hints."

"Hints aren't the truth, Mable."

"I know," she says softly.

"Do you? Because everyone keeps lying to me. They keep hiding information that would be helpful."

"We were only trying not to scare you."

"Yeah, because scaring off the girl you want to tangle in your web in hopes she can distract the spider long enough for you to get free would be a bad thing."

Mable's brows draw together. "It's not like that."

"Isn't it?"

Her eyes well with tears. "We never meant for you to be trapped here with us."

I pause and force myself to take a deep breath. Life in this town is far too short for grudges. I've seen proof of that fact already today.

"I truly am sorry I hid the truth from you," Mable says. "I believed I was doing what was right."

"Don't ever lie to me again."

"Promise." She beams at me. Then her gaze shifts to someone over my shoulder. "He believes in you, too," she whispers. "Because when he looks at you, he sees what I see."

Glancing back, my gaze locks with Sutton's as he starts toward me. "And what's that?"

"A hero."

Chapter Thirteen

"Mable," Sutton greets as he and Phineas come to a stop beside us.

"Sutton, Phineas." She grins at them both then claps her hands together. "I should be off. Books to categorize. Come see me soon?" she asks me, and I nod.

"Sure."

"Great." Then, she turns and bounds back down the sidewalk in the direction she came from.

"Everything okay?"

I turn to Sutton. "Depends. Anyone else wrapped up in your plan to bring me here?"

He pales. "She told you?"

"Yes. How did you tell her my name, anyway? If you guys were trapped apart."

"Last year's ball," he explains. "It was right before that the witch came to see me."

"And it took almost a year to bring me here."

"I didn't want to at first," he admits. "When Mable started adding your stories to the baskets they sent over the line, I decided to keep you out of it."

I stare back at him, shocked and sad all at the same time. "That would certainly explain why you didn't seem too happy to see me in the woods."

He steps closer. "I think I started feeling something for you the moment I saw your picture next to your bio."

Phineas clears his throat, reminding me that it's not just Sutton and me standing here on the sidewalk.

"This isn't over," I warn Sutton.

He grins. "I never would have expected it to be."

Clearing my throat, I do my best to shove this particular revelation down and change the subject. "Two coffees just the way you ordered."

"Thank you," Phineas says as he pulls out a cup.

"Thank you, Serenity," Sutton echoes, lifting his cup for a sip.

"No need to thank me. Jolene wouldn't even let me pay for them."

The men exchange glances that tell me I'm missing something. "What?"

"Harriet was Jolene's aunt."

Her swollen red eyes, subdued demeanor. I cover my mouth as tears blur my vision. "That's so awful."

"It is."

"I wish I would have known. I'd have—I don't know—given her a hug or something."

"Jolene's not exactly the type," Sutton tells me. "If you had tried to hug her, she probably would have shown you her teeth."

"Fair enough."

Phineas takes a drink of his coffee. "I need to run back into the station and add the coroner's preliminary report to my notes about the case. You two going to be okay?"

"You're working with the police?" I ask, surprised.

"Only until we can elect a new Sheriff," he says quietly. "With Arden gone, someone had to step up."

My chest pangs at the reminder. "Right."

"You sure you won't stay with me?" Phineas presses.

"Positive," Sutton replies quickly. "I won't risk anyone else. We'll find a place."

Phineas sighs. Sutton's comment hangs between us, and I can see Phineas' skepticism even as he turns and leaves us alone. I know he doesn't like us out here exposed like this. Neither does Sutton. Hell, neither do I. But I agree with Sutton. We can't put someone else in danger, not even if it means we're sleeping in a tent or a hotel.

An idea pops into my head, and I go with it before I can second guess myself, especially if it keeps me from sleeping on the ground tonight. Sure, I ran from the place last time I was there, but a lot has changed since then.

I've changed since then.

"I know where we can go," I announce.

Sutton turns to me.

"The B&B is empty, right? With Yvette gone—"

"No. Absolutely not," Sutton shuts it down quickly.

"Yvette is dead, though," I say.

"And Myrtle is not," he shoots back.

"Look, it's the only place available without

tenants to endanger," I say. Or, not living ones anyway.

"We've tried entering," he says. "The magic blocks our access."

"That was before," I say. He doesn't ask "before what." We both already know. "Look, we go there, see if it's unlocked, and if it is, we have a place to stay. Plus, I can finally get my own underwear back."

"I think you've been doing just fine without them," he replies, gaze darkening.

Lust pools in my belly despite the fact that we're talking about squatting in a dead lady's house, which would have made me feel like the worst person ever if said dead woman was not an evil witch who tried to kill me. "I want my stuff back, Sutton. If Myrtle is there, or it looks like she's been there, then we can leave. But you've had people watching it, right?"

He nods. "They haven't seen anything."

"See? Perfect place."

Sutton's lips flatten into a tight line, but he nods. "Fine. But if anything is off—"

"We're gone," I finish. "Promise." Here's hoping he doesn't consider the resident specters as a reason to run.

SOMEHOW, THE B&B APPEARS EVEN MORE LOOMING than it was the first time I saw it. Coffees in hand, Sutton and I walk up the driveway slowly. Jasper will join us soon along with a security detail, but for now, it's only Sutton and me. My car comes into view, and I nearly weep with joy. Rushing forward, I run my hands over the dusty paint. "I missed you, baby," I whisper.

"Did you just talk to your car?"

I glance back to find Sutton watching me, amusement on his face. "I did. What's it to you?"

He shrugs. "Not a thing. Guess I can start having my regular conversations with the coffee pot again."

Rolling my eyes, I follow him up the steps. He opens the door and peers inside. No magical wards block our entry.

"It's empty," he announces, moving inside then gesturing for me to follow.

I don't bother to ask how he simply knows we're alone here. But I can't help a twinge of jealousy. Wolf senses would be a nice perk in a moment like this one. Where my own fear makes it impossible to fully believe him until I can see for myself.

The air is stale as if the inn has been vacant for quite some time. If Yvette was hiding here, she closed herself in tight. I shiver, recalling how many nights I slept in the same house as the enemy. I'm lucky to be alive. Lucky and seriously confused about why she didn't kill me in my sleep.

"You okay?" Sutton questions.

"I'm fine," I reply, flashing him a smile. "Just weird being back here and knowing that she's..." I trail off, and he nods, knowing what I was going to say.

Footsteps on the stairs have us both whirling toward them. "I thought you said it was empty," I whisper.

Beside me, Sutton is a coiled spring. "It was."

Two people appear at the top of the stairs. When I see their faces, I exhale and grab Sutton's arm before he can attack. "Wait," I tell him. "They're not here to hurt us."

At least, I don't think so. We both watch as the couple descends the stairs and stops in front of us. Victoria claps her hands together. "Lance, look! New guests!" Still wearing her yellow puffy vest and black long-sleeved turtleneck, she looks exactly the way she did the last time I saw her. Which makes sense since she's dead.

Lance smiles softly at Victoria then turns to us. "How lovely to see you again, Serenity," he says. "I trust you've been well?"

"Serenity?" Victoria's brows draw together in confusion for just a moment before realization dawns on her. "Yes! Serenity! It is so good to see you! It's been lonely since you left. Have you seen Yvette? I was looking for her."

Awkward. "Yvette is—"

"Out," Sutton snaps. He looks torn between rage and murdery-suspicion. I get it. Victoria and Lance don't *look* like dead people. They look alive and very killable. Turns out, they're not. "You must be the apparitions Serenity spoke of."

"We prefer friendly neighborhood specters," Lance replies coolly.

Sutton shoots me a glance, and I realize up until now, he hadn't taken me seriously about the ghosts living it up like it's Groundhog Day.

"And you are?" Lance prompts.

"This is Sutton Hargrave," I say. "We're staying here until... well, until we can go home."

The word "home" sticks strangely in my mouth. It's true enough for Sutton, but for me? Where, even, is home anymore?

"Pleasure to meet you," Sutton says and extends

his hand. He seems only mildly more friendly now that he's identified Lance and Victoria, but his body is angled in front of me as if to protect me from a threat.

Lance reaches for Sutton's outstretched hand, and my jaw drops as Lance's hand closes over Sutton's. They shake, and I take notice of Lance's furrowed brow as if it's taking every bit of focus to maintain his grip.

"Are you okay?" I ask.

"Must be full of specter go-go juice," Lance jokes.

I have to bite back a smile. Okay, maybe they're not so scary after all. "Specter go-go juice?"

"Energy," he replies. "If we're chock full of it, and are able to concentrate hard enough, we can touch people, move objects, but each time we use it, the energy wanes. It's a brief way to feel human for a time."

Sutton studies Lance as if re-assessing his threat level.

"Good to meet you both," Sutton says.

Some of the tension eases, but now my attention is drawn to the rest of the house. The utter silence of it still has me on edge. I know for a fact Yvette couldn't possibly be here, but I can't rest until I see for myself that it's truly empty.

Victoria beams, clinging to Lance's arm. Somehow, they're able to touch each other? "You two make quite the handsome couple. Don't they, Lance?"

"They do," he agrees.

"We must do dinner," she announces, making my heart ache for her. How many people has she asked to dinner only to never get to follow through on the invitation?

"We're not here for dinner," I say. Her face falls, and it makes me feel like an absolute asshole. "Or at least not *just* dinner." I glance at Sutton questioningly. "But maybe we can make that work?"

She beams at me. "Wonderful! If only Yvette were here," she adds solemnly. "She makes the best roast chicken."

Sutton starts to answer, but I cut him off.

"We'll cook," I blurt out. "Tonight, I mean." I avoid Sutton's gaze, looking instead at the happy couple. "How about it?"

"Sure," Lance says.

Beside me, Sutton lets out a low growl.

"Sutton is an excellent cook," I add as much for them as for my own amusement.

"Wonderful. It's settled then." Victoria looks ready to burst with excitement.

Before Victoria can talk us into any more plans, Sutton speaks up. "Serenity and I have already had a long day," he says. "Give us some time to get settled in, and then we can talk more about dinner."

He gives me a pointed look that dares me to argue. But he's right. My skin hums with the remnants of energy still hanging around this place. I pretended not to recognize it when we walked in, but the longer I stand here, the more I know exactly what it is teasing at the edges of my awareness.

There's magic here.

More than a little bit.

It's not doing anything right now. More like the leftovers from something else. It achieved its goal, and now all that's left are the crumbs. I don't know how I can feel it, but I have a feeling killing Yvette changed more than just my body count.

Sutton doesn't react to it, and neither do Victoria and Lance. So I don't mention it. But I nod at Sutton's suggestion.

"We'll be close by whenever you're ready," Lance says, which honestly freaks me out if I think about it too hard. Can ghosts peep without you noticing?

They retreat back up the stairs, leaving Sutton and me alone. "Well," he says. "That was..."

"Creepy?"

I brace myself for some disembodied voice to complain about the insult. But everything is quiet. Even their footsteps have faded to nothing.

"So," he says, "You want to have a dinner party?"

"I want to find out what they know," I say, "About Yvette."

He looks a little more into the idea. "I'll text Jasper," he says, giving in. "Ask him to bring some groceries."

"Thank you."

"Come on," Sutton says, "Let's check out the house."

Sticking close to Sutton, I let him lead the way. Together, we wander through the first floor. Kitchen, sitting room, a tiny library, and a dining room complete the floor plan. Every room is cute and clean—and very normal looking. As if their owner wasn't a diabolical hundred-year-old witch-bitch.

We ascend the stairs slowly.

Sutton doesn't speak, probably because he's listening to our surroundings, seeking out anything that seems off. I don't speak because, if I do, my voice will probably give away my nerves.

But there's no one around.

Not in what used to be my room—which looks completely untouched since the moment I left it, right down to the dirty clothes on the floor. And not in any of the other guest rooms either.

In fact, none of them offer a shred of evidence Yvette ever lived here at all.

"This is weird," I say.

Sutton murmurs his agreement.

"Weirder than having to go through a dead woman's things," I add.

In the last bedroom, my eyes linger on a painting that is large enough to take up nearly the entire wall on my left. Its gilded frame is ornate and outdated. Something that belongs in a past century. And then there's the portrait itself. The woman looking back at us from the forest background is young and not exactly beautiful but commanding somehow with her sharp, austere nose and high cheekbones.

Her eyes are captivating. Whoever painted this was talented. It's almost as if she's looking right at me.

I turn away, shuddering at the thought. We have enough creepy creatures in this house.

Sutton meets my eyes. He wears a strange look.

"What is it?" I ask.

"Nothing." He shakes himself free of what worries him. I should press him for more, but I don't. For some reason, the idea of discussing our fears out loud in this room, in this house, doesn't seem wise.

I join him in the hall. Reaching out, he presses a rough, calloused hand to my cheek. "You're braver than you think, you know."

His words nearly mirror what Mable said to me earlier. "You really didn't know Mable was bringing me here?"

He shakes his head. "I wanted to keep you out of it."

"Even if it meant damning your entire pack? You didn't even know me."

"Ever since I saw your photo," he says, thumb stroking my cheek, "I knew I had to protect you. Even if it meant spending an eternity trapped in this hell."

"Is that your way of telling me I'm a pretty face?"

"That's part of it." He offers a smile that vanishes quickly.

"And the other part?"

"I don't know," he replies. "But I feel a pull to you. An unexplainable connection that makes me physically ache when you are not around." He leans down and presses his lips to mine. I lean into the kiss, absorbing every moment into the recesses of my memory.

Truthfully, I understand exactly what he means. Because even though it makes no sense, I feel the pull, too.

Sutton pulls back and smiles at me at the same moment my stomach growls. "Come on, let's get you some food."

He pulls me downstairs and opens the front door just as Jasper arrives with an armful of grocery bags.

"Someone call for a delivery?" he asks, a half-smile on his face.

"Thank you." I reach out and grab a few bags while Sutton gets the rest.

"Anytime. How's the place look?" Jasper asks.

"Nothing out of place," Sutton says. "In fact, we couldn't find a single personal item."

"Well, at least you have the run of the place," Jasper says with a shrug.

"It's strange, though, right?" I say. "She would have had clothes or something left behind."

"Maybe she hid her belongings," he says. "She had to know you'd get in here eventually and poke around. Maybe she has things she didn't want found."

I don't have an answer for that.

"The team's here," Jasper tells Sutton. "We're doing a perimeter check, and then we'll run regular patrols."

"Sounds good," Sutton says.

Jasper turns and heads back outside as Sutton and I reach for the grocery bags and begin unpacking.

After stocking the kitchen in silence, Sutton begins putting together some sandwiches. It's all so normal, which makes it easy to pretend—if only for a moment—that we're not shacking up in the enemy's lair with a couple of dead people as roommates.

The normalcy is relaxing, and by the time we're finished putting things away, I'm stifling a yawn. The last twenty-four hours have included little sleep for...reasons. It's catching up with me.

After topping the sandwiches, Sutton turns and offers me a plate. "Snack then nap?"

"I'm in."

After we eat, I try like hell to sleep, but it doesn't happen. Putting aside the whole "ghost" thing is a lot harder than I thought it would be. Especially when I want so badly for Sutton to get me naked, but I'm not convinced we aren't being watched.

A four-way is just not something I'm interested in. Sharing has never really been my thing.

Sutton's ringtone breaks the silence, and he offers me a smile as he answers it. "Hey, Mable." Then, he slips out of the room and into the hall.

Climbing out of bed, I stare out the window of my former bedroom, noting the security team stationed at the edges of the yard. Cara is taking a few days off, which Sutton made sound like her idea, but the hard expression he wore when he told me has me wondering if he isn't a bit irritated with her about our attack the other night. I don't ask him about it. Not because I don't care, but there simply isn't time for one more problem to solve.

My thoughts drift to Lance and Victoria.

Their presence here is another problem we don't have time for. But I can't help wondering if they aren't cursed just as much as the rest of us. Stuck in this house, doomed to repeat the same day over and over again. It sounds so … empty. Or maybe I'm thinking of my own future stuck in this damned town.

The only difference is that, for me, time marches on. For Sutton, the world stands still. Someday, I'll grow old and die. While the man I love remains the same.

My heart is too bruised to break in this moment, but it will. Eventually.

The bedroom door opens, and I turn to see Sutton watching me. I look him over in a way I haven't done since before this nightmare of a day started. He's wearing dark jeans and a shirt that clings in all the right places. The stubble dotting his jawline and the wild, unkemptness of his hair thrill me. My stomach flips at the sight of him, at the way he watches me like I'm the center of it all. I still can't understand how the hell my hormones can continue working in the middle of all this chaos. But they do not seem deterred in the slightest that sex as a priority makes zero sense.

Lust is a nonsensical little she-devil.

"I'm going to the library to give Mable a hand with the questionnaires," he says.

My sexy daydreams are splashed with cold water. "Oh."

"Give me a hand?"

I bite my lip. "Help with the interrogations?"

He arches a brow. "You don't approve?"

"It's not that. I just... I'm not sure I'll be of much use. I don't know these people like you do." I take a deep breath and add, "I think I need to take some time to work on my magic."

Words I never thought I'd say.

He nods as if it's the most normal idea in the world.

I don't bother to mention the fact that I've been feeling its pull stronger than ever since the moment we stepped foot in this house. Or that I'm mostly concerned with the fact that I killed a woman last night, by accident if we're being technical. And I damn sure don't want that to happen again. Especially with someone I care about. Someone like Sutton.

He hesitates, clearly debating the wisdom of my proposal.

"Don't look at me like that," I say. "I'll be fine."

He doesn't look convinced. "You have half a dozen wolves stationed outside, right?"

"Yes." He doesn't look satisfied. "I'll call for a few more. And two on each door."

I roll my eyes but don't argue. Not when I think about reversing the roles. He almost died last night, and I can still taste the panic and absolute devastation I felt in that moment. I don't want to put either of us through something like that again. Even if it means a whole army of babysitters.

"Fine, but you have to take your own entourage too," I say.

He seems to understand my thinking and nods. "Deal."

I meet him in the doorway, and he pulls me into his arms. I wind my arms up and around his neck, clinging tightly. For a moment, I let myself forget what waits for me outside the safety of his embrace. All that matters is Sutton's heartbeat against mine. My hands release and slide down his chest. Underneath my palms, I can feel the rise and fall of his chest.

He bends down and steals a lingering kiss.

When it's over, he presses his forehead to mine, his eyes closed.

"Be careful," he whispers. "I can't lose you."

I pull his mouth back to mine, my lips meeting his like a promise. "You won't."

Chapter Fourteen

With Sutton gone, the silence is deafening. I half-expect Victoria and Lance to pop up and invite me to dinner again or compliment my hair, but they're nowhere to be found. Their absence is eerie now that I know they never actually leave these grounds. The longer I stand around thinking about it, the creepier their non-presence becomes.

I look down at my hands, noting their heaviness.

The magic clings to them as if attracted like a magnet. The more I use it, the more aware of its presence I've become. It seems almost unbelievable that, up until a few weeks ago, I didn't know I was capable of magic. And now, since last night, I can't stop noticing how much of it my body contains.

The only disconnect has been how to access it deliberately. But now, I have a theory.

With a deep breath, I concentrate, calling to the parts of myself I tapped into before—when I used it on Yvette. The fear that fueled my determination. The desperation. The depth of my desire to protect my loved ones.

Emotion, overwhelming and nearly uncontrolled, wells up inside me.

Without warning, blue sparks shoot from my fingertips. A bolt of magic hits the vintage lamp beside my bed and sends it crashing to the floor, shattering the glass top into tiny pieces. I flinch then press my hand to my mouth to keep from screaming. Something about the noise against utter quiet is terrifying.

Shit. "Sorry! I knocked something over!" I call out, hoping it's enough to keep the guards at bay. Given their exceptional hearing, the last thing I need is one running into the room in the midst of a magical panic attack.

Rushing forward, I stop again when my feet crunch over the broken shards. I step back and look around, trying to think through my racing thoughts.

Emotion. That's the key. Except, if I can't control my feelings, how can I possibly hope to control my magic? Unfortunately, the only other magic user in this town is intent on destroying us all. Not exactly someone I can go to for lessons.

My search for a broom and dustpan leads me downstairs. I poke around the kitchen and closets and am elbow-deep in a pantry full of canned goods and cleaning supplies when I hear a voice behind me.

"Have you decided on a menu for dinner?"

I jump, hitting my head on a shelf, and stumble backward into the kitchen. My hip bumps the large kitchen island, and I nearly topple over. Straightening, I stare at Victoria, wide-eyed and full of adrenaline. Beside her, Lance shoots me an apologetic look.

"You nearly gave me a heart attack," I say, still catching my breath.

"Sorry about that." She pauses. When I start to move away, she holds up her hand. "Don't go!"

I halt.

Her shoulders sag. "I'm just glad for company. It gets lonely here."

"Oh." Of course it does. Once again, my heart pangs in empathy. What must it be like to be a ghost with no friends? "Okay."

I move away from the pantry and look between

them. If I'm going to share this place with them for the foreseeable future, I might as well get to know them. And maybe see what they know about Yvette in the process.

"So, how do you like Midnight Falls?" Victoria asks brightly.

"It's … different."

She grins knowingly.

Lance steps forward. "This might be easier if we lay our cards out a bit. We understand the residents in this town are … a bit more than human."

"I see. Yes, that does make it easier." I don't know why I feel weird outing a bunch of supernatural creatures when Lance and Victoria are otherworldly beings themselves. "In that case, the real answer is this town is unlike anywhere else I've ever visited," I admit.

"We totally agree," Victoria says. "From the moment we arrived, we knew something was different here. Didn't we, sweetie?"

"There was a certain feeling about this place," Lance agrees.

"Were you two… I mean, before… were you human?" I ask.

"Yes," Lance says. "We were human."

"We didn't know about the wolves here either,

not until after we died," Victoria says. She frowns. "And even then, it's been a bit of a roller coaster re-learning the truth all the time."

"You mean the memory loss," I say tentatively, but she just laughs.

"Yvette keeps things so hush-hush, but there's no need. Hell, I don't know I'm dead half the time sooo," she shrugs, "Your secrets are safe with me."

"Was that a thing before you died?"

"Umm, not to be funny, but I don't remember," Victoria admits, her expression completely serious.

I should probably win an Oscar for keeping a straight face at what is clearly not a joke—but also totally is.

"No," Lance answers for her. "The memory loss came after. Part of the trauma, I think, of our crossing over to this side of things."

"And the whole Groundhog Day thing?" I ask.

"It's Groundhog Day?" Victoria's eyes widen.

"Well, for you, I mean, with the whole repeating thing..." I trail off, realizing the repetitiveness is probably just due to Victoria's short-term memory and not actually repeating the same day over and over again.

"It's true," Lance says. "Every day feels much the same. We can't leave the property, and we have no one else for company other than the residents of this house."

"That must be hard," I say. "I wish there was a way to help free you from this loop. Give you back your memories. Maybe you could even move on or whatever."

"We're together," Lance replies, taking Victoria's hand in his. "Who knows where we'd be if we weren't here."

"Yeah, but, what if you could be together somewhere that's not this lonely house?"

Lance looks at me sharply, and I can tell he knows something's up with Yvette's absence. He doesn't ask, though, and I don't offer it. Not until I'm sure they aren't going to haunt my ass for eternity as punishment. For all I know, they were all besties.

Victoria smiles softly at Lance. "We're soulmates," she tells him. "No matter where we go, we'll be together."

He gazes lovingly at her. "I just want to be with you."

My eyes prick with tears. Their love, it breaks my heart. Those who claim love is easy are wrong. Things with Roscoe? They were easy—for a time. But then, that wasn't true love. I know that now.

With Sutton, things are never easy. We are creatures from two different worlds on a collision course. The stronger my feelings become, the harder it gets to imagine a future where we're together and happy.

As for Victoria and Lance, their love wasn't even given a chance before they were robbed of a future. It's heartbreaking and incredibly unfair. While I understand Lance wanting to stay with Victoria, what comes next has to be better than this endless loop, right?

"Do you really think you can help us?" Victoria asks. "A change of scenery would be nice," she adds, more to Lance.

He frowns but doesn't argue.

"Maybe. I mean, I'm happy to try." I may not have been able to break the curse, but surely helping a couple of ghosts move on is something I can manage. After all, there are fewer stakes with this one, right? And if I can help them, then perhaps it will atone for at least some of my failures.

Even if I know they will weigh on me for the rest of my life. However long that might be.

"Do you have time now?" Victoria asks, eyes lighting up.

"Sure, I—"

"Your husband left," Lance says; a statement, not a question.

"He's not my husband." My cheeks heat, and I look away.

"I see. You're here alone then."

For some reason, the way he says it puts me on edge. I straighten, squaring my shoulders. "There are men posted at all the doors. Probably listening and watching right now."

"Forgive me, I only meant..." He exchanges a look with Victoria, who seems to actually know what he's thinking. "We want to show you something."

"Okay," I say.

Victoria claps her hands in excitement.

"This way." He leads the way back upstairs, and I follow.

As we walk, I notice the way their feet click against the floor—the sound is so corporeal. It's weird. Part of me wants to ask them how it works, becoming solid and then... not. But before I can figure out how to do it without insulting them again, Lance stops in front of a door at the end of the hall.

"In here," he says.

It's the room at the end of the hall. The one with the larger-than-life portrait from earlier. I follow him inside, purposely averting my eyes from the woman on the canvas.

The magic is thicker in here. My skin tingles with it.

"Not much to see in here," I say, mostly as an excuse to hurry up and get the hell out.

The vibe in here is "creepy Victorian chic," and I'm not here for it.

"No," he agrees. "Yvette hid her personal spaces well."

That gets my attention. I watch as he crosses the room and opens a wardrobe.

"Hid?" I echo, confused.

He doesn't answer except to retrieve something from the wardrobe. He turns back to me and holds out a thick, leather-bound book.

"Where did you find it?"

"There. A false bottom." He gestures to the wardrobe shelf and I look from there back to the book he's holding out.

"What's this?" I ask.

He hesitates. I glance from him to Victoria, whose cheeks have gone pink with some sort of embarrassment.

"What's going on?" I ask.

"We heard you," Lance admits. "Earlier. With your— With Sutton."

"What did you hear?" I ask, instantly wary. Were they spying on us, after all? Gross. We're going to have a talk about boundaries.

"You've come into your magic," he says. "And you need help controlling it."

My eyes narrow. "What the hell do you know about my magic?"

He smirks, the little shit. "You're not the only one we've heard inside these walls, Serenity."

My heart beats a little faster. "Yvette."

He nods. "We know she wielded magic. And that you do too."

"We heard her talking about you," Victoria admits. "On the phone."

"What did she say about me?"

"At the end, she was afraid of you. Afraid of what you might be capable of. It must mean you're very powerful." He glances at Victoria again. "You said before that you wanted to help us. Maybe this book can help us all."

The book. Right.

I look down and brush off the dust that's begun to gather across the cover. Underneath is a symbol. A five-point star inside a circle. My hands tremble as I trace its lines. I suck in a breath and crack open the cover. Inside, Yvette's name is scrawled on the first page. I flip through, surprised to see most of the pages are blank, like a journal. The ones with writing are handwritten, and I can only assume Yvette herself put this together.

"What is it?" I ask, scanning some of the entries she left behind.

They read like instructions.

"She called it a grimoire," Lance says.

I look up at him sharply. There's no trace of deception, but then again, I'm not an expert on dead people's facial expressions.

A grimoire. I've watched Charmed enough times to know that basically means this is a witch's spellbook. If so, maybe Lance is right. Maybe Yvette left enough instruction in these pages to teach me how to use my magic.

I page through, faster now, scanning for some entry that's about me or about magic in general. Harnessing it, controlling it, maybe even getting rid of it. I don't necessarily want to give up the one thing I have to defend myself, but I also can't afford to harm anyone I love with it either. However, there's nothing quite as obvious as all that.

Instead, the pages are filled with specific spells

ranging from simple to complex. How to bring a plant back from the brink of death. How to glamour an item by hiding it in plain sight. How to conjure a cat. The further I go, the more complex the spells become.

Maybe learning how to do some of these will help me understand my magic. If nothing else, practice makes perfect. I stop on a page titled "Release the Soul" and scan more quickly.

"Ooh, what did you find?" Victoria asks, noting my interest.

She comes to stand over my shoulder, and I try not to react to the fact that I can see her plain as day but there's zero sensation of physical presence. Not even a brush of her shirt against my arm. Apparently, her energy level is at zero.

I will never get used to this.

"Release the soul and set it free, As I will, so mote it be." Victoria sings the words like it's a child's rhyme, but my entire body reacts with an awareness that leaves me breathless and swaying on my feet.

The magic in the room seems to ripple.

I look from her to Lance. "This is it," I say. "If I can do this spell for you, maybe it'll free you from being stuck here."

A faint flair of hope lights in Lance's eyes. Victoria squeals and jumps up and down, clapping her hands in excitement. "Oh, that sounds so fun," she says. "Then maybe we can go to that fancy dinner place."

Lance's expression softens as he looks at his wife.

"And maybe it'll restore her memories," I say quietly. "For good."

He nods, expression tight. "Let's give it a go."

Lance helps me find and gather the items listed. A candle. A bowl full of water. Chalk. Every one of them is hidden inside this room. False bottoms in the drawers. A loose floorboard with a hole underneath. I have no idea how they just know where things are. Nothing better to do than spy on Yvette, apparently. I don't think too hard about it, though. I'm too busy reading over the instructions so that I'll feel mildly prepared for what I'm about to do.

Then again, what can possibly prepare a girl for her first spell?

Yvette's words are clear and concise, and I'm weirdly grateful. With such clear instructions, hopefully not much can go wrong. Still, I can't help worrying I'm about to send the future into some twisted version of itself. This isn't Practical Magic,

I remind myself. I'm not manipulating anyone. I'm doing a good deed. Offering inner peace or whatever.

Following the spell's instructions, I use the chalk to draw a circle around me and the items I've gathered. Halfway through, I catch sight of the painting again and pause, wishing we'd picked a better location. Above me, straight ahead, hangs the woman whose eyes still seem to follow my every move. But we've come this far. I'm not going to derail us because of some dumb painting.

With a steadying breath, I begin.

The words are simple, the steps straightforward. I light a candle then dip my finger in the bowl and let it drop onto the floor. Then I recite the words. Over and over again until the magic that lingers in the room begins gathering itself to me. My hands grow heavy. Full of energy. Finally, a spark lights underneath my skin. The floor creaks, and the furniture shakes, and I have to swallow a scream because, hello, this is the kind of shit horror movies are made of.

Lance and Victoria step to the edge of the circle and join hands. Victoria grins at me. Lance looks desperate with hope.

There's a sound like something ripping, and I look past the ghostly couple to the painting.

The canvas has been torn in two. The halves hang loose now, blowing in the creepy-ass wind that gusts through the room. The problem isn't the fact that it's torn itself open, though.

Panic lodges in my throat as I realize the woman in the painting is gone.

Footsteps sound behind Lance, and he whirls, moving aside to reveal the absolute creepiest fucking thing I've seen yet. The woman from the painting is solid and alive—and standing directly in front of me.

Lance takes one look at her, and he and Victoria vanish.

My jaw drops.

Holy shit.

They just...did that.

I turn back to the woman. Holy shit, *I* just did *that*.

Her mouth curves in a smile that looks faker than a pair of newly purchased knockoff knockers.

"Well, can't say I expected you to do me that particular favor," she says haughtily, smoothing her dress and patting her hair as if she's just freshening up rather than coming to life. "But thank you, all the same, I guess."

I pick my jaw up off the floor long enough to ask, "Who the hell are you?"

She cocks her head as if surprised I don't already know the answer. "I'm Tabitha Augustus. Sutton's fated mate."

Chapter Fifteen

I stare at the ghostly form standing before me. You have got to be fucking kidding me. This cannot be real. I close my eyes, picture her gone, and open them again—only to see that she's still here and wearing the same sadistic smile from moments before.

Son of a mother fucking crackerjack. Did I help Victoria and Lance move on? No. Did I summon Sutton's ex-girlfriend? Fuck yes, I did. No, not even a girlfriend. His crazy, obsessed, psycho stalker and the very reason this entire town was cursed in the first place.

How the hell do I keep making things worse? I swear, if ever there were an award for situation escalator, I would win the grand prize, hands down.

I clear my throat. "It's, um, nice to meet you."

"I'm sure." She grins at me then begins to move about the room, her old-fashioned heels clicking against the hardwood floor. "I have to say, I'm quite surprised you are the one who freed me. I never would have expected aid from you, Serenity."

"How do you know my name?"

"I know quite a bit about you." She glances back at the ripped painting. "Wasn't much else to do but listen to my aunt gossip with my mother."

Aunt. Mother.

She means Yvette and Myrtle.

She's telling the truth.

My gaze travels to the torn canvas then back to her, and I groan. No fucking wonder Sutton was caught off guard by the woman in the painting. The last time he saw her, she was dead.

Sutton. He is *never* going to leave me alone again when he realizes I accidentally summoned his stalker.

"How are you here? *Why* are you here?"

"You summoned me," she replies, almost aggravated she has to explain it. Well, excuse the fuck out of me. Summoning spirits is not exactly something I do every damned Tuesday.

"And what does that mean, exactly?" I ask.

With an eye roll, she explains, "You freed my soul from the confines of that bloody painting." She spits the last word. At my raised brows, she explains, "Mother has a sick sense of humor when it comes to punishments."

"Are you saying your own mother killed you then imprisoned you in a piece of wall art?"

"Are you doubting her cruelty?" Tabitha demands.

"Not at all. Only her ability."

I've been a victim of Myrtle's handiwork for long enough. Still, what Tabitha is suggesting tops everything I've experienced so far. Then again, if I was ever tempted to feel sorry for this girl, her answering snarl squashes it.

"My mother is incredibly powerful," she says, rage contorting her expression. Then she blinks, and her anger cools, replaced by a calculating suspicion. "But so, it seems, are you."

"Whatever, look, you're free now. Move on. Go into the light or however it works."

She cocks her head to the side and studies me with scrutiny. "Why would I do that?"

"Because you're dead."

"That is nothing but a small hurdle for a love as true as mine." She moves across the room, gliding elegantly toward a writing desk in the corner. My gaze drops to the sharp letter opener gathering dust.

Can she hurt me?

Victoria has occasionally touched me…Lance shook Sutton's hand. What if—"True love knows no limits," she coos. Her fingers pass directly through the letter opener, so I breathe a sigh of relief. Seems you have to be dead-alive for a hot minute before you get that particular party trick.

"Love?" I snort, feeling a bit less threatened now.

Her eyes darken, and she bares her teeth. "I saw him kiss you earlier."

Oops. Here's hoping ghost bitches can't throw hands. "And your point is?"

"Sutton is not yours."

"He's not yours, either."

Tabitha snarls, her eyes glistening with the challenge I'm apparently giving her. "You truly have no idea what you've gotten yourself into, have you?" Moving forward, she stops mere feet from me, right on the edge of the chalk-drawn circle.

And since I'm not one to back down from a challenge—a personality trait I'm seriously starting to see as a flaw—I get to my feet and stand my ground. "If you're trying to intimidate me, it won't work."

"Intimidation?" She barks out a laugh. "There is no need to intimidate you, witch, because you don't have a chance with him. He is mine. It has been written so."

This bitch is crazy. Straight up fucking nuts. Bonkers. Elevator doesn't go to the top floor. Lights are on but no one is home. "Isn't that the kind of psycho-babble that got you killed in the first place?"

"Did you ever hear the story of how I met my love?" she questions, tone almost wistful as though revisiting a happy memory.

"You mean the story of how you became obsessed with a man who never wanted you?"

She arches a perfectly shaped dark eyebrow. "Never wanted me? Is that so?" Tabitha bites down on her bottom lip and smiles, making my skin crawl. "Our paths crossing was not mere coincidence, little witch."

Good, we can add condescending to the crazy. "Oh, no?"

"In my family tomes, a prophecy was written. I stumbled across it in my studies of our ancestors. It was a long entry, a list of prophecies that had already come to pass about our family line. I'd tried my best to ignore it more than once, uninterested in boring historical accounts. But when I finally sat down to read it, I realized the end of it held a future prophecy; something that hadn't yet come to pass. And that prophecy was about me and Sutton."

"Give me a break," I say, rolling my eyes.

She ignores my interruption. "'The true mate of the Hargrave Alpha is the daughter of my line,'" she quotes, and my stomach drops.

The fuck?

Tabitha goes on while I wrap my head around what she's saying. "Since his father was already mated, it was simple enough to realize it was the son mentioned rather than the father. After all, he was destined to be Alpha, was he not?"

She begins to pace, and I watch her with wide, desperate eyes. I can't possibly let myself accept her crazy-ass claim.

"Even if what you're telling me is the truth, it could have been anyone in Sutton's line," I say. "Could have been Sutton's great-great-grandchild it referred to." I cling to that because surely she is *not* the true mate of *my* Sutton. She can't be.

"I considered that. But I was curious, so I went out looking. I waited in the woods outside their manor, watching, biding my time until, finally, he stepped out. So handsome." She stops pacing and presses both hands to her heart, practically swooning. "It was then I *knew* he was mine. It was then that I gave him my heart."

Okay, time to bring out the big guns to shut this insanity down. "I hate to break it to you, but Sutton never loved you."

Her eyes harden, and the floor beneath her feet creaks as if she's actually influencing physical reality with her anger. "He would have. But his mother..." She trails off, a snarl on her lips. "That bitch kept getting in the way."

I very much doubt that, but antagonizing an already insane ghost seems like it wouldn't be the smartest of ideas. "And why did she keep doing that?"

"I sent him letters, but his mother always intercepted them. She hid them so he wouldn't see."

"Sutton saw those letters, Tabitha. Hell, I've seen them."

She glares at me. "Those were not meant for you." And she completely glazes over the fact that I just told her Sutton did, in fact, see the letters. And that he chose to ignore them.

"You made a mistake," I tell her. "You misread, misinterpreted. It happens. In fact, I suggest you check out a movie called, He's Just Not That Into You. It might explain some things."

"I did not misinterpret," she hisses. "I am Sutton's fated mate. I am his, and he is mine. The great Seers of my ancestors foretold it."

"No—"

"I certainly hope you enjoyed your time with him, witch. Because it is over."

Below, a door slams. "Serenity?" Sutton calls out, and I freeze.

Tabitha lights up like a fucking bulb at the sound of his voice. Then, she turns to me. "I'll be seeing you soon, Serenity. Thank you for my second chance."

She disappears the same way Victoria and Lance did, leaving me staring at the place she vacated. Sutton's footsteps thud on the stairs as they carry him closer to me.

Oh fuck.

Oh shit.

What the hell am I going to do? Attempting to buy myself more time, I rush out into the hall before he can see the destroyed painting and chalked up floor. He looks exhausted. Completely and utterly worn down, which makes me feel even more like shit.

Because I'm about to make it a whole lot worse.

"How did the interrogations go?" I ask, the sound of my voice more high-pitched than usual.

He sighs. "I don't know why I expected them to yield anything. They never have before as I understand it."

"I'm so sorry."

He shrugs. "Eventually, she'll have to show herself. I just hate not being able to do anything. Inaction drives me mad."

Ugh. Wait 'til he hears about *my* action.

"How's Phineas?"

He looks physically pained. "Frustrated. Listen, until we know for sure who we can trust, it's just us, Serenity. You and me. We're the only ones we can be sure are not Myrtle."

"You think she's taken your dad?"

"I think anything is possible. And I want to be even more careful from here on out. We should have been cautious from the beginning. I never should have let you go out without me." He pinches the bridge of his nose.

"I took care of myself."

"But you shouldn't have had to." He moves forward and opens his mouth to speak again but then closes it again as his gaze drifts past me to the door I left open. Eyes narrowed, he walks into the bedroom. The moment he turns to the destroyed painting, his body tenses. "What the hell happened in here?"

"Listen. Before you get mad—"

Sutton whirls on me. "The guards said they heard and saw nothing out of the ordinary, which means I know this wasn't an attack—or was it?" He rushes forward. "Are you okay?"

"No, not an attack." *At least, not a physical one. I did, however, get a mini lashing for having my tongue down your throat.* "I'm fine. Promise."

Sutton crosses his arms. "Then what the hell happened? What is this symbol drawn on the floor? Why is the painting destroyed?"

"So you know how Lance and Victoria are stuck here?"

"Yes."

"Well, Lance brought me up here to show me where Yvette kept her belongings." Bending over, I retrieve the book of spells I dropped onto the floor. I show it to him, but he doesn't reach for it. "He showed me this. It's apparently a—"

"Grimoire," Sutton finishes. "All witch families have them."

I decide not to hate on him for knowing something I didn't.

"Yes, well, there's a spell in here to free a trapped soul."

Sutton's mouth falls open, and he gapes at me. "Tell me you did not practice magic when you have no idea how to actually use it?"

"How else am I supposed to learn?"

"For fuck's sake, Serenity!" He throws his hands in the air and turns away from me for a moment. When he faces me again, he's more composed. "Please tell me you were at least successful. Tell me that we're the only ones in this house now."

I bite down on my lip. "I mean, the spell did technically work."

"Serenity."

"I might have accidentally freed a soul I didn't mean to free. But to be fair, I didn't know she was trapped!"

He looks about two seconds away from losing his shit. A bomb about to go off, Sutton stares at me and then looks at the painting. It's when his gaze returns to me that his face loses color. "Tell me it's not her. Please, for the love of everything, tell me you did not free the same woman who was in that painting."

"Tabitha says hi." My attempt at a joke is completely pointless, and I hate myself for making it the moment the words leave my lips.

Sutton explodes. He whirls around and slams his fist into the wall. The wooden boards crack beneath the strength of his hit and he turns to face me. Chest heaving, he takes one deep breath then another, finally gaining composure. "Tabitha's alive."

"Not alive, exactly. She's a specter like Lance and Victoria." He glares, but I keep going. "She was trapped in that painting. Apparently, it was her punishment from Myrtle for causing all of this. Which, by the way, you could have mentioned it was her when you saw it!"

"So, this is *my* fault?"

"No. That's not what I'm saying."

"Fine." He forces out an exhale, but I can tell it's not helping him calm down. "You freed her. And now she's what—gone?"

I wince. "Not exactly."

"You do realize that you just set loose the soul of a woman who has more reason than Myrtle to want you dead, right?"

"I do realize that, yes. And obviously, had I

known it was a possibility, I wouldn't have done it!"

Sutton shakes his head and closes his eyes for a brief moment. "She is a ghost, correct?"

"Yes."

"And she didn't harm you, which likely means she can't."

"No. I don't believe so. At least not right now."

"But at some point, it could be a very real possibility." His gaze narrows on me.

"Yes."

"Shit, Serenity." Sutton takes a deep breath. "Her not attacking you means she's an annoyance, not a problem. At least, not yet." He sighs. "Are you okay?"

I don't even mention the prophecy, though it stays in the back of my mind. I don't want to believe it, but I'm a reporter, which means I also know my denial doesn't make it false.

No. Tabitha is nuts. There is no way it's the truth. It can't be.

"I'm fine," I lie. "Just a bit shaken. Not every day you run into the ex-stalker of the guy you're sleeping with." Sutton looks unconvinced, but there isn't anything either of us can do about it now. "So, how about that dinner with our friendly neighborhood specters?"

Chapter Sixteen

Dinner with Lance and Victoria is strained. No one wants to talk about Tabitha or my failed attempt to help free my ethereal friends. To be honest, I'm surprised they showed up after bailing on me the moment Tabitha popped off the painting.

Either way, it's an awkward evening, and before we've even made it to dessert, I feign a headache. We end the night early with a promise to do it again soon. Something that'll probably happen sooner rather than later since, chances are, Victoria won't remember any of this tomorrow anyway.

Though, at least, they had time to confirm our suspicions. All Tabitha needs is to re-generate her spiritual energy and learn to concentrate. Then, she goes from annoyance to threat. Yet another problem we need to deal with.

As Sutton and I clean up the kitchen, it's all I can do not to jump out of my own skin every few minutes.

So far, Tabitha hasn't appeared, and I can only hope she stays away. But my movements are jerky, my nerves frayed, as I wait and wonder for the moment she'll pop up.

Sutton's silence feels deliberate. I'm still not sure where we stand after our argument earlier, but I can't stop thinking about what Tabitha said. And I can't stop wondering if she's listening right now.

A moment later, Sutton's arm brushes my elbow, and I yelp, dropping a clean plate back into the soapy water.

"Sorry," he murmurs then peers sharply at me. "You okay?"

"Just a little jumpy," I admit.

He frowns.

"Let's go upstairs," he says, taking my hand and pulling me toward the stairs.

"But, the dishes," I begin.

"I'll finish them tomorrow."

With a sigh, I let him lead me up the stairs and into our bedroom. I hesitate, unsure about changing when it's highly possible I have an invisible audience. Sutton's crumbling manor house sounds cozy as hell right about now. At least there, the only occupants are corporeal.

Sutton, apparently, doesn't give nearly as many fucks about it. He sheds his clothes and crawls beneath the covers, motioning for me to do the same. I change quickly into an oversized shirt and sleep shorts and join him, grateful for the warmth of his body.

He wraps his arms around me, holding me close, and I breathe him in, shutting out everything else.

"I'm sorry I yelled at you," he murmurs against my hair.

I melt a little. "Me too," I whisper. "It's not your fault."

"It's not yours either." He strokes my hair. "We're going to figure this out, Serenity. And I will keep you safe, I swear it."

There are so many reasons to poke holes in that promise, but I don't. Instead, I shut my eyes and pretend he can hold up his end. Just before I drift off, I swear I hear soft laughter echoing through the walls.

A HARD BODY PRESSES AGAINST MINE, SCOOTING IN close to spoon me from behind. I'm not even fully awake as I scoot reflexively closer to the hardness pressing against my ass.

"Mmm," Sutton hums, his voice low and delicious against my ear.

His arms tighten around me so there's no space left between us at all.

My desire wakes me fully, and I tense against him. His hand, moving lazily over my hip, stills.

"What is it?" he asks.

Oh, nothing, just the idea of your crazy-ass ex-stalker watching us has me drier than the Sahara.

"I just … can't," I say, my own blue balls leaving me irritated at myself for those two words.

But Sutton just relaxes and continues to cuddle me. "It's okay," he says quietly.

I can feel how very much it is not okay, but I'm grateful he lets it go. The minute I stop caring whether ghosts watch me climax is probably the minute I join the crazy-pants category along with so many other residents of this town. Then again, if Sutton keeps waking me up like this, I'll probably give in sooner rather than later.

The man has a way with his hands.

Finally, he peels himself away to shower and

dress. I groan, hating myself for my own sense of propriety, but the longer I'm left alone, the easier it gets to think about something else besides Sutton's chiseled abs and impressive... gifts.

Inevitably, I think of Myrtle. And Tabitha. And how much I need to figure out a way to stop them both. Or, at least, lift this curse that has me trapped here inside their personal brands of torture. But the more I consider leaving, the harder it is for me to see a future for myself anywhere other than Midnight Falls. Or with anyone other than Sutton Hargrave beside me.

My gaze drifts to the door where he's showering. And I realize—what if he's not alone in there? Jumping out of bed, I rush toward the door and open it before scanning the room for any ghost bitches. While there is nothing but steam, I do notice a shape appearing on the mirror as if someone drew it there before the shower came on.

Stomach full of rocks, I move forward and glare at the single heart drawn on the mirror. I didn't do this, which means ghost bitch did.

"Coming in to join me?"

I glance back at Sutton as he peers around the curtain, hair wet, a grin on his face. "I think Tabitha was spying on you."

He looks to the mirror and arches a brow. "Maybe you should come in to protect me."

It takes me a moment longer than it should to realize he's messing with me. My nerves dissipate, and I fight the urge to punch him. "You asshole."

But Sutton's grin is worth every moment of misplaced anger. "You are the one who released her, darling. Consider that payback."

"Definitely not getting in there with you now," I reply with a grin as I turn and saunter out of the bathroom, shaking my ass with a bit more effect than normal.

Take that.

Nearly ten minutes later, Sutton re-emerges, dressed and ready for the day—whatever it holds. I watch from the bed as he gathers his things and puts on his shoes.

"You're leaving?" I ask.

"I'm going to check in with Mable. See if she has any books that might help us un-do your, uh, trick yesterday."

"Okay."

"Join me?"

"Maybe later. I'm going to read through Yvette's grimoire and see if there's anything I missed. I promise not to attempt anything until you get back," I add before he can argue.

He nods. "The security teams are doubled up just until I get back," he adds. "Will you be okay?"

"I'll be fine." I have a house full of ghosts watching my every move. "Not like I'm alone here."

He bends toward me and presses a kiss to my forehead. "Be careful."

I frown as he walks out, knowing full well he means I shouldn't try any more magic while he's gone. The fact that he's probably right irritates me enough that I form an idea. If I can't use Yvette's grimoire, that means I need a different sort of teacher. And if Myrtle, Tabitha, and Yvette are all from the same family line, and they are all witches, that means it's very possible there's another witch in my family too.

Reaching for my phone, I dial the one person who might know something. She answers immediately.

"Serenity!"

"Hey, Mom. How are you?"

"Me? How are you? I was beginning to wonder if you fell off the face of the earth."

I cringe. "I know, I'm sorry I haven't been great about keeping in touch."

"It's okay. I just want you to focus on yourself for once, sweetie. You deserve that after everything with, well, you know."

"You can say his name, Mom. Roscoe."

"Right. I didn't want to upset you."

"Believe me, I've gotten past it."

"So I hear." The smile in her voice is evident, and I groan. Steven.

"Ugh, what has that bastard told you?"

"Your brother simply mentioned that you met someone. I think it's great, honey. Truly. Even if it's just a passing—what do you kids call it?—rebound bang."

"Mom!" My cheeks flush, and she laughs into the phone.

"Seriously, honey, I am happy for you."

"I cannot believe you just said rebound bang. You've been listening to Sawyer too much."

"I'm no prude, my dear. How do you think you and your brothers got here?"

"And now I might vomit."

She laughs again, clearly proud of herself. "So, this time away has been helping, I take it."

"I'm focusing on myself," I say, using her words

because it's safer than trying to describe what's actually going on.

"I'm so glad. You deserve all the happiness, sweetheart."

"Thanks." I take a deep breath. *Here we go.* "Hey, can I ask you a question?"

"Anything."

"Well, I have a friend who is kind of into the whole genealogy thing, and she thinks her ancestors were involved in the witch trials. Do we have anything like that in our family line?"

"Witch trials, wow, that's interesting."

It's a horrible lie, but it's the only one I could think of that wouldn't raise a red flag with her. My dad is a total history buff, so this, at least, will feel semi-normal to bring up.

"I'd have to ask your father but—"

"Ask me what?" his muffled voice echoes through the line.

"Oh, hold on." There's a shuffling sound, and then the audio changes a bit to sound hollow. "You're on speaker, dear. Now what was the question?" my mother asks.

I repeat my rehearsed lines, and this time, my dad answers. "I'm not aware of any witch trial affiliations," he says. "Our people came over from

Ireland sometime in the nineteenth century, so I think we missed out on all that. What's your friend's family name, and maybe I can dig something up."

"Oh, you don't have to do that," I say.

"Your father thrives on these things, Ser, you know that," my mom says.

"It's just a silly idea," I say, "nothing to trouble yourself with, seriously. I just loved the idea of a real witch in the family."

I laugh it off, my attempt dry, but my mother is way more amused. She chuckles hard enough to make it clear she thinks this is weird and says, "Someone's been binging Charmed again."

"Right." I sigh, forcing out a response that will placate her and end this topic. "The reboot isn't the same."

"It never is," she agrees.

For some reason, her words hit me like a punch in the gut. I tell them I love them and hang up the phone. In the silence, all I can think about is my mother's response: *It never is*. Her words echo in my head, haunting me long after the call is ended. I turn the words over in my mind, trying to figure out why they're bothering me so much.

Finally, I realize with a sad jolt, it's me.

I'm the reboot.

Trying to pretend I'm as good or better for Sutton than Tabitha. But what if that prophecy is right? What if she really is his fated mate? I've read about mates before. Mostly fiction novels like Julie Trettel or Jaymin Eve. In those stories, every single mate is a destined pair. No one can tear them apart, not even a magical curse-casting bitch with the power of a hundred years in her hands.

Not even me.

My chest pangs, and the ache I feel is a bleak acceptance.

I want to weep for myself, for the loss of a man I never really had to begin with. I can't help but lick my wounds and silently curse Tabitha for being the cause of my heartbreak. That makes twice now I've lost the man I cared about to another woman. I won't make it three.

Maybe for me, love is off the table.

Maybe it was never on the table to begin with.

The only thing I have left is my magic. And even without a destiny that involves Sutton and me together, I know I can't forsake the people of this town who've been cursed. Nor can I sit back and let Tabitha haunt me forever—literally and physically.

If anything, her presence here only makes me more determined to end this curse and get the hell out of this place forever. If I can't have Sutton, I have to walk away. Living here with him every day, knowing she's the one who's meant to have him, is a torture worse than anything Myrtle could do to me now.

I have to master my magic. I have to break free. And I have to say goodbye to the only man I've ever loved. Battling a witch is one thing; battling fate is another.

SUTTON DOESN'T COME HOME FOR LUNCH. HE CALLS to check in, and I can hear the worry and strain in his voice. Mable has nothing helpful for learning about my magic. But I know that's not the worry he fears most. It's been two days since Myrtle killed Harriet and used her blood to reset the wards. Two days of waiting for whatever it is she's going to try next. The longer she remains silent, the more worried he gets.

And the more desperate I feel to learn something that might help.

I shower and then settle back into bed with Yvette's grimoire. If nothing else, it can offer insight into the mind of a witch—even if she was batshit crazy. At this point, the list of who isn't insane in this town is shorter than the list of who is.

But two hours later, my eyes blur with exhaustion and I've learned nothing helpful. Sure, I could probably cast a spell to conjure a black cat, but none of the spells listed here can actually defeat someone like Myrtle.

I'm out of ideas and, I have a feeling, nearly out of time.

A creak sounds somewhere in the house, and I jerk toward the bedroom door. It remains closed. No more sounds follow. My heart thuds, and I brace myself for someone to just pop up in the middle of my room. But no one appears.

"Fuck this," I grumble and toss back the covers.

The moment my feet touch the floor, a single sheet of paper flutters before me. I snatch it out of midair, angry at the way Tabitha is clearly taunting me with her presence.

"What the hell is this?" I demand.

No answer.

I scan the paper, expecting a death threat or some other thinly veiled psycho-babble. But it's not. In fact, it has nothing to do with me at all. My heart sinks lower as I read it once then a second time, trying to convince myself I've misunderstood. But there's no mistaking the words printed on the page. I turn it over, noting the handwritten scrawl on the other side too.

Tabitha's family name.

Augustus.

Dated the eighth of January, 1745.

"I have seen many things with the Sight of the Goddess. Here be one. An Augustus daughter fated to mate a Hargrave son. The alpha must choose his own destiny, but beware, son of beasts. If you refuse her, you will be destroyed by your rejection. The only way to be truly whole is if you accept the love freely given."

It's a journal entry of some sort.

Written by a woman named Constance.

And maybe I would have chucked it straight into the garbage if it didn't confirm Tabitha's screwed-up claims about Sutton being her mate.

The longer I stare at the words on the page, the sicker I feel.

Another creak sounds. This one from the hall. She's close, that bitch. Laughter echoes off the walls, and I snap. Folding the paper, I stuff it into my pockets and lace my shoes up. If Tabitha can't leave, I will. I'm getting out of this house. Now.

Chapter Seventeen

For the first time in what feels like forever, I run.

My shoes hit the soft ground with barely audible thuds as I move through the trees, my arms pumping. Behind me, the security team follows—close enough that I feel safe but far enough they can't see the tears steadily streaming down my cheeks.

All of this is too much.

I never wanted to carry the weight of the world on my shoulders. I was content with my little slice of life. But now that I've tasted Sutton? That I've become a part of something so much bigger than myself? How the hell am I supposed to go back to normal?

How am I supposed to move on without him?

My chest tightens, a vise that steadily squeezes the life from me.

A few miles in, I realize I have no idea where I am anymore. Glancing back, I see the security team still keeping up. Pressing on, I leap over a small fallen branch and push out into a clearing.

Removing the earbuds from my ears, I gape at the huge waterfall just ahead. It spills down into a crystal pool of water that laps softly at the bank. The sound of water roaring as it crashes drowns out even the heavy beat of my own heart.

I take note of the security team just inside the tree line before moving closer to the water and taking a seat. Drawing my knees to my chest, I tuck my face and do something I almost never do—I cry.

I cry for the woman I was, the naïve, heart-broken woman who ran away from her pain and straight into a nightmare. And I cry for the love I found here, love that will never amount to anything more than time well spent.

It can't.

Tabitha made me see that.

Even if we find a way to break this curse and free ourselves from Myrtle's torture, Tabitha's prophecy will remain. The fact is Sutton's destined for someone else. Maybe it is Tabitha, maybe not. But it's not me. And I refuse to hold him back from his true destiny.

This has to end. Now or later.

A hand goes to my back, and I sniffle, blinking back more tears. Sutton's scent fills my lungs as he sits beside me, remaining silent.

My mom always told me that crying was okay. That falling down was normal. But that once you do, you have to pull yourself back up. *Do not remain on the floor, Serenity,* she'd tell me. So, after a few moments, I take a deep, steadying breath, and lift my face to look out over the water.

"I forgot how beautiful this place is," Sutton says.

I glance around and realize the security team has vanished.

"Where are the others?" I ask.

"I sent them away."

His strong fingers trail down the side of my face before he grips my chin and turns my face so I look at him. His hazel eyes are full of questions—that much is easy enough to see. Gaze narrowed on my face, he strokes my cheek. "What is it? Did something happen?"

Pulling away from him, I shake my head.

"Then what is it?"

Shoving up, I get to my feet and cross my arms to keep the traitorous limbs from reaching for him. My chest constricts, my throat burning with emotion. "Did you know there's a prophecy written about you? About your mate?"

His jaw tightens, telling me all I need to know.

"You did," I whisper. "You knew, and you let me—" Closing my eyes against the tears, I try to keep at least a slice of composure amongst the heartbreak. "You knew," I repeat.

"It's a bunch of bullshit." He steps toward me, and I retreat.

"No."

"Serenity, Tabitha used that to try and draw me in. My mother—"

"So your mother did have a hand in keeping you apart?"

"She didn't want Tabitha to use it as a way to manipulate me into a relationship I didn't want. It's a lie, Serenity. Just like everything else she says."

"Tabitha certainly believes it's true," I tell him, and he turns away for a moment, muttering something under his breath I cannot quite make out.

He turns back to me, pain and accusation in his eyes. "So something else did happen."

"Actually, Tabitha filled me in on the fact that she is destined for you yesterday."

"Now who's keeping secrets?" he shoots back.

"It's not a secret if you already knew it."

"There's no proof—"

"Oh? Then what's this?" Reaching into the small pocket on my leggings, I withdraw the folded piece of paper. "Go ahead, Sutton, take a look."

He takes it from me and carefully unfolds it, his expression hardening as he reads the words scrawled on the paper. The words that cement what Tabitha has been telling him.

"Do you have any idea what this means? If it's true—"

"It's not!" he roars, crumpling it in his hands. "It's not true." But I can see the hesitation on his face, the brief instant in which even he is questioning its validity.

"If it is, though," I choke out, "You denying her could be what is causing all of this."

"Myrtle is causing this," he snarls back.

"Sutton. It says right here that rejecting your mate will destroy you. I can't be the reason you die." Tears spill from my eyes, slipping down my cheeks. "I can't go through this, I can't—"

"There is nothing between Tabitha and me," he

urges, moving closer. His hands grip my arms, and he rubs them gently. "The prophecy is not true. It's made up. We know Myrtle is behind all of this."

"But what if it's not all her? What if part of the reason you're being punished is because you didn't choose your true mate? That paper says you will be destroyed if you refuse but whole if you accept."

"*You* make me whole, Serenity."

I shake my head, refusing his words. "The prophecy says your mate is someone from the Augustus family line, so it can't be me. Don't you see?" I choke out, gesturing between the two of us. "This is doomed."

"You don't believe that. Tabitha is wrong. That prophecy is nothing but a bunch of lies written by a troubled woman. Hell, she might have forged it!"

"She's not corporeal, Sutton. There is no way she could have written it."

"Then Myrtle—"

"Hasn't been in the house," I choke out, poking holes in all of the logical explanations he tries to throw my way. "And Tabitha. She would never write something that would push you together. "

"Tabitha could have written it before she died."

"Maybe. But how do you know? Is it truly worth the risk?"

"You are worth every fucking risk, Serenity. There is not a damn thing I wouldn't give up for you."

"In that, we agree. Because I will give you up if it means you survive."

Sutton throws the paper to the ground and closes the distance between us. My eyes flutter closed as he cups my cheek. I wish I could freeze this moment, preserve his touch. "You are who I want, Serenity. Not her. It's never been her." His lips press to my cheek as he kisses my tears away.

My heart breaks.

Shatters.

Explodes into tiny little jagged shards that pierce me to my very core.

"I love you, Serenity."

Tipping my face up to his, I see that he truly believes those words. And, who knows, maybe he does, but I'm not going to fall for this trap again. If Sutton and Tabitha are truly meant to be together, there is nothing that will keep them apart.

"Please. Believe me."

More time. I need more time. Or maybe just one last time, a final goodbye. So, tipping my face, I stretch up and press my lips to his. Sutton's large hands go to my hair, removing the band holding it back and threading through the strands.

I breathe him in, wrapping my arms around his neck as I taste him on my tongue. Kneeling, he takes us both to the soft ground beside the water. It roars, drowning out all sound. For a little while, I'm going to let it drown out reality too.

Sutton's hand slips beneath my shirt, his fingers scorching my flesh as he drives the fabric up, pulling away from me long enough to remove it from my body. Cool air hits my bare skin, and his eyes darken as he takes in the sight of me.

A moment later, he reaches down and strips his own shirt off, tossing it aside. He stares down at me, his masked expression giving nothing away. Chest rising and falling with heavy breaths, he crawls over me, lowering himself against me until his lips trail down my throat to my breast.

I moan, arching up as he draws my nipple into his mouth. Pleasure shoots through me, warmth burning through my body like a rogue flame. Yet, even as I am loved by him in this moment, the tears flow down my cheeks because I cannot help but remember this can't last.

Sutton's mouth trails up my face, and he presses his lips to my cheeks, kissing the tears away as he palms one of my breasts. Loving him has given me the best moments of my life.

And those are what I will cling to. Pushing him off of me, I stand, my gaze locking with his as I undo the laces of my shoes, slipping out of them before peeling my leggings from my body. Within moments, I stand before him, completely bare.

A low growl leaves his lips and he moves toward me, remaining on his knees to press a kiss to my stomach. My hands tangle in his hair as his warm breath fans over my skin.

"You are everything, Serenity," he whispers, staring up at me through thick lashes.

I swallow hard but don't speak, terrified that the words won't come out even if I try.

Sutton stands, slowly, then frees the button on his jeans. He pulls them off and then stands bared beneath the late afternoon sun.

If I can ever only have this moment—I'll take it. A greedy treat to myself.

We clash, skin on skin, his hands are everywhere as we drop to the ground again. I climb onto his lap as he sits up, one arm wrapped around my back. Holding his gaze, I lower myself onto him, pleasure shooting through my body as he fills me.

Sutton's lips part, and he swallows hard as I

move—up and down—slowly. Drawing out every single moment I can, I torture the both of us with delicate movements. Here, surrounded by trees, we steal peace in the midst of chaos. Life in the presence of so much death.

And when Sutton leans in and kisses me, the tenderness confirms what I already know—this has to be goodbye.

For the safety of him and his entire pack.

We have to walk away.

Chapter Eighteen

Sutton doesn't comment on my silence as we get dressed. I can feel him watching me, trying to catch my eye, but I don't look over. Not even when I retrieve the torn page from where he threw it on the ground earlier and stuff it back into my pocket. What happened between us just now changes nothing. I don't want to argue about it anymore. The truth just is.

We head back the way I came, though I barely recognize the path from earlier. Sutton seems to know the way, and I let him lead me, telling myself it's the logical reason for letting him hold my hand. And why I cling to his in return.

"Mable and I spoke today," Sutton says, breaking a silence that's only getting more tense as we go. "She has an idea for a way we can lure Myrtle out. Set a trap. Go on the offensive instead of always playing defense."

"This sounds promising," I say. The sooner we end this and put it behind us, the sooner I can move on. Or try.

"We use the painting idea," he says. "If she found a way to lock her own daughter inside it, maybe we can do the same to her."

"You told her about Tabitha?" I ask, cringing.

"The pack needed to know."

"You told the entire pack?"

"We're all on the same side, Serenity."

I think of George and wonder how true that statement really is.

"Even if we wanted to, we can't. The painting is destroyed," I tell him.

"So we get another."

I decide not to point out that magical paintings probably aren't that easy to come by. Not that I would know. But if it were that easy, every portrait in the world could potentially be home to a ghost.

That thought makes me shudder.

"And who will you get to perform the spell?" I ask.

He cuts me a pointed look, and for some reason, it pisses me off.

"I'm nowhere near skilled enough for something like that," I say.

"How do you know? You brought Tabitha back from it. Who's to say you can't do the opposite if you tried?"

"Where is this coming from?" I ask. "Yesterday, you made it clear how reckless it is for me to do magic without understanding how it works. And today, you want me to just blindly go for it."

"What I want is for this curse to end," he says.

"So do I," I say, but the words feel hollow. When it ends, what then? What will I do? It's not like I have a job to go back to. That's long gone. And so is any semblance of a life I might have had back in New York. I can't even imagine trying to be happy in that city anymore—and that scares me just as much as being trapped here.

"Your sparks haven't burned me in days," he adds, and I jolt with surprise.

He's right. About that, at least. Since that night with Yvette, my magic's been just a bit easier to access—and easier to control.

I'm getting better at it, after all.

"I believe in you, Serenity. You're the curse breaker. Now you just have to believe in yourself."

I don't answer.

His words tug at me. It feels unfair, this push-pull we have with one another. Even if I refuse to give in to my feelings toward him, we're still connected. That has to mean something; I just have no idea what. Or if it's enough.

Sutton lets me have my thoughts. We walk in silence, and I try to pull myself back from the dark turn my mood has taken.

When Sutton's hand tightens suddenly, I look up sharply. One look at his intense expression and I know something is wrong.

"What is it?" I ask.

He's staring at something off the path. I follow his gaze to a pile of fur half-buried underneath the leaves.

Dread slams into me along with recognition.

That's not just a pile of fur. It's a wolf. Or the body of one, anyway.

Blood cakes its face and throat. And more blood stains the ground nearby.

"Is that—?"

"Jasper," Sutton says tightly. "Yes."

"Is he...?"

"I sense no heartbeat."

We both scan our surroundings, suddenly more alert. But if the threat is still here, I can't sense it.

"Come on." Sutton pulls me down the path, faster this time.

I have to nearly run to keep up with the strides of his longer legs.

But then, he's pulling me up short again.

I see it right away this time.

Another wolf, bloodied and still among the brush.

"Lyall." Sutton's voice is low. Full of grief—and rage. I don't have a chance to answer before he turns and nods at a third wolf. "And Salvador."

"The team," I realize. The wolves who'd followed me out here.

Sutton sniffs, attention darting left and right.

My heart thuds wildly.

We continue on, and in another horrifying few moments, I spot Fischer and Damon too. The entire security team—all dead. And we didn't hear a thing.

Guilt threatens to consume me right here, but Sutton's hand squeezes mine, pulling me along like a lifeline.

"Where are we going?" I ask.

"I need to get you back to the house," Sutton says. "Then I can call for the pack to—"

"Leaving so soon?"

I let out a short scream as a woman steps out from behind a tree. Sutton yanks me behind him but not before I see her face—and nearly vomit at the sickening familiarity of it.

"Audrey," I breathe.

"Hello, Serenity." She inclines her head. The move is jerky, unnatural. Which makes total sense because the woman standing before us, skin sagging like a pair of last century's tits, is dead and gone.

Except that she's here.

And alive?

What. The. Fuck.

"Myrtle," Sutton growls.

His body strains toward her. I can feel the indecision in him. He wants to attack her, but he won't tear himself away from me.

Judging from the smug smile she wears, she knows it too. "Yes, Myrtle is close by, but she's not inside me, not anymore."

Horror fills me at what she's implying. What I'm actually seeing.

It can't be.

It's impossible.

"What is this?" Sutton demands.

"A little reanimation spell." Her gaze zeroes in on me in some kind of silent challenge as she adds, "Nothing a seasoned witch can't handle."

Reanimation?

So it *is* possible.

"Do you mean this bitch is a zombie?" I nearly shriek.

Audrey-Myrtle offers a smug smile—as if my horror is a testament to her greatness. "That is one word for the magic, yes," she says. "A magic I can show you how to wield if you let me."

"Lady, you are crazier than a witch's tit. I want no part of your kind of education."

Sutton bends down and picks up a fist-sized stone. Before Zombie-Audrey can react, he hurls it at her. The rock strikes her on the cheek. It rips away a chunk of skin but otherwise does no damage. She doesn't even seem to feel it.

I grimace at the disgusting reveal of cheekbone.

"That was unnecessary," she says.

I actually happen to agree.

"What do you want?" Sutton demands.

"Serenity," she says as if it's obvious. "I thought I made that clear the night of the ball."

"I will die before I let you hurt her," he says.

"Intriguing idea," she says, "Especially considering the debt she owes for taking my sister's life." Her eyes narrow at me. "Your magic is powerful, city witch. More than even I imagined." She looks at me so intently I can almost feel the energy between us. "Tell me, what's it like?" she asks softly.

"It's..." I don't know how to answer. Or why she wants me to.

The truth is, it's empowering as hell. Just like that night in Sutton's library during the ball, I am drawn to the power of magic like a moth to a flame. But something about that truth feels too much like giving her what she wants.

"It's a handy little weapon," I say, "Especially against witch-sisters who fuck with my friends."

Audrey opens her mouth and screams.

The shrill sound is more than human. It's supernatural and hurts like hell. I cover my ears, wondering whether my eardrums will burst. But Sutton's answering growl is loud enough to match it, and a second later, Audrey falls silent again. Her jaw closes, but the hinge seems off.

"What the hell," I demand.

"Your betrayal pains me. My sister was important. But..." She pauses as if gathering self-control.

Honestly, the woman moves like a puppet on a string. She's a skin sack, controlled by magic. It's disgusting. "What's done is done. If you agree to help me now, I will agree to peace between us."

"Help you," I say warily. "What could you possibly want my help with?"

"The magic necessary for the curse is no small thing."

"Are you saying your own magic isn't enough?" I challenge.

"I am more than powerful enough," she scoffs. "But your magic would make an excellent replacement for mine. And it would be enough to cast this curse permanently in my absence."

My jaw drops at the fucking audacity. "You think I'm going to help you curse these people? A spell that has also trapped me? You really are insane."

"It's true, you are trapped, but that's not what pains you most, is it, Serenity?"

Her words are sharp and knowing—and they slice me into silence.

"You and I both know the real pain is being forced to spend eternity with someone you can't have. Someone you aren't meant for." Her gaze flicks to Sutton, and he growls, but Audrey cuts him off. "I can take that pain away. If you let me, I can show you how to keep from ever feeling that kind of hurt again."

She pauses, confident in her offer. She thinks she has me. And honestly, what she's promising is tempting. A release from the hurt at letting Sutton go? At loving him and then walking away from him —forever? I'd be lying if I said I didn't want that.

"How?" I ask, and Sutton growls again.

Audrey ignores him. "Magic, of course."

I bite my lip. "And in exchange, what do you want from me?"

"Your blood," she says.

"What if I say no?"

"Then I will take what I want—by force. And you may or may not survive the experience."

Beside me, Sutton growls.

"I will have what I want, Serenity. One way or another."

"And I will fight you every step of the way," Sutton snaps.

"I have no doubt." She looks from him back to me again. "You can save him the heartache of losing the rest of his family in the process."

I can feel Sutton's eyes on me. I look over and let him see the temptation to give in written in my expression. He turns away, and when he does, it leaves a hollowness in my heart. This woman is offering to put me out of my misery—but at what cost?

No matter how much it hurts to love Sutton Hargrave, I won't save myself by cursing him. I will die a thousand painful deaths—or worse, live a thousand painful lives—if it means freeing the man I love from the grip of this crazy-ass witch.

"Yeah, I think I'm going to pass," I say.

Sutton's eyes whip to mine. Relief shines back at me, followed by fear. "She'll try to kill you," he warns.

"Emphasis on try," I tell him. Then I look back at Audrey whose cheeks have actually reddened with rage, which is kind of impressive, given the deathly pallor that clings to her. "You do what you gotta do, lady, and I'll do the same. But I will never, ever come to the dark side and help you."

Stuart would be quite proud of my Star Wars reference.

Audrey's eyes flash with barely controlled fury. "You will regret your choice, Serenity Kellis. If you won't offer me what I want, I will come and take it."

Audrey takes a step forward, but Sutton steps in front of me.

"Stay back," Sutton snaps at her. His chest heaves with labored breaths, his muscles straining against what's left of his control. "You won't harm her, not without me ripping you apart in the process."

She holds up a hand, her face blank of any emotion as she stares back at Sutton.

"Despite my desire for vengeance, the only one I'm interested in hurting," she says, eyes gleaming as her voice builds, "is you."

The last two words echo around us. As if Myrtle herself is speaking them through Audrey's decaying mouth. As if another mouth has joined the chorus.

The eerie echo ends as another woman steps out from behind the tree.

Sutton stiffens beside me. His reaction is worse than any I've seen. Worse even than finding his entire team dead in the brush. I look closer at the woman, trying to figure out who she is.

Her few remaining strands of dark hair are combed into an up-do my great-grandmother might have worn, and her old-fashioned dress and high collar are reminiscent of another era. Then there's the fact that her exposed bones are covered with very little skin. Even the dress' fabric—now riddled with holes—hangs off her bony shoulders like it would a hangar. Whoever she is, she's clearly been dead a long time.

Beside me, Sutton lets go of my hand and falls to his knees, his expression twisted in anguish.

"Hello, Sutton," she says.

"No," he chokes out.

"Sutton," I say, bending down to check for some unseen injury.

He only stares at the woman, more pain in his gaze than I've ever seen. It ignites a protectiveness in me that warms the magic swimming underneath my skin.

I let go of him and straighten, glaring at the woman. "Who are you?" I demand.

"Forgive my manners," she says with a jaw that creaks as it moves. "I'm Vivian Hargrave. Sutton's mother."

Chapter Nineteen

Vivian Hargrave? Is this chick for real? All the color drains from Sutton's face as Vivian shifts her attention from me to him. "Son. Just as I remember you."

"No," he growls, his fingers digging into the soft soil at his knees. "You're not her."

She ignores his accusation. "How is your father?" she questions. "I do miss you both." She sniffles, but the darkness in her eyes only deepens, the corner of her mouth lilting in amusement at Sutton's obvious pain. "You would reject me? Just as you rejected your own mate?"

"That's enough," I snarl, moving in front of him. "You are not Vivian."

Her grin spreads, a smile far too wide to be human. "But I am. Aren't I, Sutton?"

"We need to go," I urge Sutton.

He doesn't move. "We have to save her."

"Sutton..." I try to keep my voice as gentle as possible because my words certainly aren't. "I'm sorry, but that's not your mother. Your mother is dead, and you know it."

"I'm right here, Sutton." Vivian opens her arms. "Come give Mommy a hug, won't you?"

Sutton makes a pained sound.

I whirl on him and reach down to wrap both hands around his biceps. I try to tug him to his feet, but the difference in our body sizes is enough that the struggle is very, very real. Unfortunately, the magic I feel gathering around us is also real. Something tells me Myrtle's patience with this little game is about to end.

"Dammit, Sutton, get up," I hiss.

Something hard hits me square in the back, and I lurch forward, tumbling over Sutton and falling to the ground. A large stone lands beside me, and Sutton's control snaps. He shifts. Turning from man to wolf in a mess of torn clothing. Then, turning his face to the sky, he lets out a bone-chilling howl.

Hopefully, that means it's time to go because I am fucking done here.

Myrtle's apparently done, too. Playing nice, that is. Out of the corner of my eye, I see movement, and when I squint into the trees, I see what she's brought with her to take this to the next level.

More bodies.

Dozens, at least.

They're moving slow, but they're coming this way, every one of them disjointed and clearly … undead.

Apparently, Sutton's mother wasn't enough of a mindfuck.

This bitch has an army of zombies headed our way.

Despite the pain radiating from my back, I climb to my feet and take off at a sprint, Sutton directly behind me. Myrtle, wherever she is, sends magic aimed sharply at our heels. Jumping over tree branches and small fissures opening in the ground at my feet, I race, arms pumping, lungs burning. Twigs snap around me as more of the dead stumble through the trees, a sea of unknown faces all rushing toward us.

Shit.

My heart hammers in my chest as adrenaline

surges through my veins—the only thing keeping me going as I race through a legitimate zombie attack. I saw I Am Legend and had nightmares for weeks over those undead assholes. Who the fuck would have thought I'd be right in the center of my own version of the story? Except, no virus created these fuckers. Unless you count Myrtle. That woman is a disease, for sure.

I stumble through brambles, zig-zagging past fleshless hands. They reach for me, bony fingers outstretched, and I barely make it through their lines without being torn to shreds.

Up ahead, the bed and breakfast comes into view, and hope blooms in my chest as I notice the crowd waiting for us there. The yard is packed with townspeople, and as soon as Sutton lunges through the tree line they shift. At once, dozens of humans change to wolves, their clothes flying in all directions as their bodies transform—twisting into their animal. Predators, every one.

They snarl but hold their ground. I glance behind me to the dozens of undead now at our backs and then nearly stumble in surprise as Sutton suddenly shifts back to human.

"What are you—?"

"We have to hurry." He grips my hand and yanks me back toward the B&B.

"Sutton! Let me go!"

"I can't focus if you're not safe," he roars, his naked body covered in dirt and a sheen of sweat.

"But they want *me*," I say, desperate to help fight. The thought of letting anyone else die for me is a crushing weight.

"That is exactly why I need you to wait inside. Serenity, please."

Maybe it's the zombies closing in on our heels. Or maybe it's the pure desperation in his dark, stormy gaze, but I give in and let him drag me toward the front door.

"If you think I'll leave you to deal with them alone, you're dead wrong," I shoot back as soon as we're inside the house.

Victoria and Lance pop into view right in front of us, both of them wide-eyed. "What is going on?" she questions, but my attention is on the man currently trying to hide me away when I should be in the middle of the fight.

"You cannot be out there, Serenity. You can't defend yourself like we can."

"I have magic," I argue, "or have you forgotten?"

"Have *you* forgotten that it's *your* blood she needs to seal us away forever?" he growls. "It's *you* she's after. So stay the fuck here, or you risk trapping us all."

I know he's right.

He knows he's right.

Dammit.

"Help her hide," he orders Lance. When he turns to leave, I know I cannot follow. No matter how badly I want to be out there. Who knows how much blood that bitch needs. A drop? Easy enough for a fucking zombie to get.

The door slams, and I turn to race for the stairs.

"Serenity!" Victoria calls out. "You need to hide!"

"No!" I yell back as I throw open the door to my bedroom and race for the window overlooking the yard. The dead line the trees while the wolves stand, ready to fight. Sutton's wolf—easily discernable from the rest thanks to his massive size—moves to the very front of the crowd, right next to a slightly smaller gray wolf I imagine is likely Phineas.

Phineas. Oh no. I cannot even finish the thought before Vivian herself steps from the trees.

He drops his head and whimpers before trying to move closer. Sutton blocks his way, and my heart shatters. It's horrific enough to lose the person you love, but then to be forced to see them as your enemy— Myrtle is going to die for this.

"We've come for the blood of Serenity Kellis," Vivian says, and I'm not sure which is worse—her demand for my blood or the fact that her husband and son have to watch this grotesque animation of a creature who looks like—but isn't—the real Vivian Hargrave.

"You will leave without it—or you will die," Sutton says, his voice hoarse at the threat he's just tossed at the remains of his own mother.

She doesn't answer.

I clench my hands into fists and hold my breath as moments tick by.

And then, like a scene straight out of a war movie, they clash together.

It's chaos. Bodies moving too fast for me to keep up. Frantically, I scan the crowd for Sutton. Behind me, Victoria gasps, but I ignore her, my eyes glued to the scene below. Limbs and body parts fly as the wolves tear the dead apart—but not without casualties of our own. A white wolf— soaked in blood—falls to the ground as a trio of skinless women move on to another target. Their weapon? The pointed ends of their own bony fingers.

I press a hand to my mouth and will myself not to be sick. "This is bull shit. I can't stand here and do nothing!"

"Who says you have to do nothing?" I turn to Victoria, who gestures to the heavy history book on my nightstand. She tries to pick it up, and her hand passes right through it. "Throw the book at them," she declares before glancing at Lance with a cheesy smile. "I've always wanted to say that."

"Book? I can't throw the book!" But then my eyes land on the ceramic bookend right beside it. "Now *that* I can throw." Crossing the room in two strides, I retrieve it then rush back over and yank the window open. Leaning out, I scan the crowd for the closest victim—and find them. Directly below me, a dead man trots toward a wolf not paying attention, so I wait, one, two, three seconds until—I let it go.

It falls to the ground, crushing the skull of the already-dead guy.

The thing crumples, and I grin. "Who says I can't help?" I ask, turning to Victoria with a triumphant smile.

She grins at me. "Again!"

I scan my room for another makeshift weapon. But it's not the physical items I notice most now. Magic permeates the air around me, infecting my blood with potency, and I let it, embracing it instead of my usual attempt to ignore it. If I can throw something physical, I can certainly do more. Especially since I seem to be powerful enough to warrant an entire zombie army.

Giving in to my emotions, I channel it all into the magic, closing my eyes and imagining striking down the zombies below.

When I open my eyes, I wave my hand toward them—but nothing happens.

No blue spark.

No zap of electricity.

My heart falls.

"What is happening?" Victoria questions.

"I don't know." Throwing my hand out like the Scarlett Witch in every Marvel movie, I expect to see *something*, anything, but instead, the zombies and wolves continue to battle it out, un-effected by my magic.

It stings far worse than I care to admit.

A sharp howl echoes from the thick of the fighting, and I shift my gaze in time to see Sutton face off with his mother—or what used to be his mother.

Vivian's smile is crooked, and the dress she wears is now hanging limply over her left arm. As if chunks of her limb are now completely gone. My stomach roils.

This is wrong. This is all wrong.

I turn and rush out of the room. I'm nearly down the stairs when Lance pops into view. I yank to a stop to avoid passing through him. Could I? Yes. But something about it seems...rude.

"You can't go out there," Lance insists.

"You can't stop me," I remind him.

"Sutton—"

"Sutton is currently engaged in a fight with his very dead, very decayed mother."

Victoria materializes with a gasp, and Lance's eyes widen.

"I will not leave him to face her alone," I add. "I can't."

Still, they don't move. I sigh. *Screw manners.* Running straight through them, I race down the stairs, outside, and directly into the fray. Almost immediately, I duck as a body is thrown past me and into the side of the house. Bones crunch, but the thing—I honestly can't tell if it was a man or woman at this point—gets right back up and charges toward the wolf who tossed it.

From here, I can't see Sutton through the chaos. I sprint toward where I saw him last, rounding the corner of the house, but a man steps into my path, blocking me. His uniform is wrinkled and covered in mud, dimming the shine of the badge still pinned to his lapel.

He grins, his familiar face looking completely alien to me now. His throat is missing patches of skin where it was cut to bleed him the night of the ball. And his eyes are hanging way too loosely in their sockets for my liking. I take a step back, unable to breathe at the sight of him. Probably a good thing because, up close, he smells like death.

"Hello, Miss Kellis," Sheriff Arden Rhodes says. "So nice to see you again."

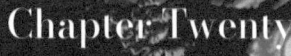

Chapter Twenty

I stare in horror at the man whose death I've carried as my own failing since the moment it happened. Guilt settles against my shoulders all over again, but my disgust makes it hard to feel sorry. The fact that he's standing here at all is just ...wrong.

"Get out of my way," I say.

"I died because of you, and now you won't even spare a moment to speak with me?"

"You died because of Myrtle," I retort, ignoring the way his words stab at me. "She's the reason all of this is happening." I force myself to look him in the eyes and add, "I know you can hear me, Myrtle. Stop this. These people have done nothing to you."

"This town took everything from me," he hisses.

From the venom and disgust in his words, I have no doubt this is Myrtle I'm speaking with now. "First my daughter and now Yvette. They deserve to suffer as I have."

"You killed your daughter. Not these people. Not Sutton."

"It would have never happened without his involvement. The Hargrave family is a blight on this world. And now they feel the pain they caused me."

"Tabitha started this, but you can end it. Right now."

"So can you. Give me what I want. Your blood. And I'll go. Forever."

"You'll trap us forever, you mean. Just like you trapped your daughter."

"What do you know about Tabitha?"

"I know she's free now," I say. "Thanks to me."

"What are you talking about?"

"I found the painting," I say. "Or should I say 'prison'? What kind of mother doesn't let her own daughter's soul find peace?"

His eyes narrow and I know I've hit a nerve. Myrtle clearly didn't realize Tabitha's been let out to play. Rhodes casts a glance toward the house. I can feel Myrtle's desire to go see for herself. Good.

That means my distraction is working. While I buy myself time, I gather what magic I can to myself, but like before, I can barely pull enough together for a single spark.

Dammit.

"She's still determined to have him, you know," I go on. Rhodes looks sharply back at me again. "Even after all this time, she's chosen him over you. Why do you think that is? Oh, maybe because you're the villain here. Not Sutton and not any of these people."

"You're wrong. These people are rabid animals," he replies. "And what do we do with rabid beasts, Serenity? We put them down."

"The only rabid one I see here is you," I spit back. Casting my gaze behind me briefly, I catch sight of the book stopper I threw out the window. I take a step backward toward it. "Using your victims as glorified meat puppets? Pretty fucking twisted."

"But it sure is a show stopper, is it not? Oh, come on, as a writer, I assumed you of all people would appreciate the theatrics. The plot twist as it is."

"I write non-fiction, you bitch." Reaching behind me, I retrieve the bookend and swing out. It slams into the Sheriff, ripping chunks of flesh from the side of his face. His head whips back toward me, and he reaches up, snapping his dislocated jaw back in place.

I gape in horror, the urge to vomit nearly overwhelming me.

"You pathetic little girl," he growls. "You truly have no clue just what you are doing, do you? Use your magic, Serenity. Go on. Show me what you're made of."

He reaches for me, and I stumble back, going down hard on my ass. My fear surges, and I let it loose. Magic shoots from my hands but it doesn't hit him. Instead, the shot flies wild and hits another zombie square in the back. The undead drops where it stands, crumpling and turning to dust in an instant.

Rhodes lunges for me, and I scramble to my feet, barely managing to escape before his hand has a chance to close around my throat. He grins, a savage smile that is so out of place it makes the bile churning in my belly rise to my throat.

What she's doing to these people—it's wrong on so many levels.

"Go on, Serenity," he taunts. "Hit me with your best shot. I'm waiting."

I reach for my magic and thrust a hand out, but nothing happens.

He laughs. "Pathetic. Give me what I want, and I'll go away," he says.

Somewhere behind me, a wolf whimpers, but I'm too afraid to look away to see who it is. *Please don't be Sutton.*

I bite my lip, fully aware I'm out of options for self-defense. "If I give you my blood, you'll leave and never come back?" I ask.

"You have my word," the Sheriff replies.

The word of a murdering, necromancing witch.

Like that means anything.

The offer is almost tempting, though. *Almost.*

"The word of a psychopath doesn't mean shit," I say.

With my magic on an unapproved vacation, I do the only other thing I can think of. I raise my leg and kick. My heel hits him square in the chest. Bones crack, but despite the horrifying sound, he is completely unaffected. Instead, he grabs my ankle and smiles as he yanks me forward.

A scream leaves my lips as I'm pulled from my feet. My head hits the ground, pain ricocheting through me as the injury leaves me dazed. Everything around me fades, the sounds of fighting coming through as if I'm underwater.

My arms scrape over the ground as Rhodes drags me closer to him. Then, he kneels. I throw up my hands to fend him off, but my movements are too slow. He grips my arms and pins them above my head with one massive hand.

Then, he reaches behind him and withdraws a silver blade. It glints beneath the light of the sun as he shows it to me. "You will beg me for mercy," he growls as his shriveled hand tightens its grip. The cold, dead fingers bruise my wrists as he leans down with the blade.

A menacing snarl pulls my attention as a massive wolf slams into the Sheriff. The two tumble to the dirt, and the wolf jumps to his feet, his gray fur matted with blood—and chunks of things I really don't want to think too strongly on.

Blinking rapidly, I manage to sit up, my head pounding.

Sutton's wolf gnashes its teeth as it stares at the Sheriff, who is already pushing to his feet.

"I will have her," Rhodes growls. Then, he charges.

So does Sutton.

The two clash, Sutton taking Rhodes back to the dirt.

Sutton brings his claw down and rakes it across the Sheriff's face. Skin shreds, falling away to reveal bone and tissue. But the Sheriff continues to struggle, and Sutton responds by sinking his teeth into Rhodes' throat and ripping it clean away.

Thick, black blood bubbles slowly from the wound. Not much. Hell, not nearly enough for him to seem alive though he continues to act like a newly dying man. His breath catches, and when he coughs, the dark crimson leaks from his mouth too.

Gross.

Sutton growls and closes his mouth around the Sheriff's throat again. He shakes his head, jerking the body until his neck snaps. The cracking sound it makes brands itself in my mind, and I know, without a doubt, it's a sound I'll remember for the rest of my life.

Finally, the Sheriff stops moving.

He's gone. A second time. Hopefully for good, this time.

I press a hand to my mouth as nausea rolls.

Sutton steps back, positioning himself in front of me, but there's no need. The rest of the zombies have already begun to retreat; what little there are left of them. Nearly all are lying dead—again—in the soft grass where the remaining wolves still bare their teeth at the ones animated enough to move.

"This isn't over," I hear a disembodied voice call out as the remaining zombies disappear into the trees. I cannot do anything but look at the dead Sheriff and try not to vomit. Bile rises as the adrenaline begins to wane, sending my body into uncontrollable shivering.

Sutton kneels in front of me, human once again. His naked skin is covered in blood, soaked in it. The overwhelming stench of death clings to him, and I scramble back, covering my mouth with one hand. He reaches for me, and I shrink back further, unwilling to be touched by the blood of a man I've seen die twice now.

"Serenity," Sutton says, his voice rough with emotion. Worry, pain, relief—it's all there, but I don't know what to say to any of it. "Serenity." He calls my name again, this time rougher. His tone almost pleading with me to assure him that I'm okay.

Truth is I don't know if I ever will be.

Finally, I look up, but my answer is cut short by a crack of thunder.

No, not thunder.

I know that sound. And it means something much, much worse than a bolt of thunder.

"Get the fuck away from her, or the next one will be between your eyes."

Cold familiarity washes over me as the last voice I ever expected to hear in this cursed place registers. I whirl to see Steven behind me, the barrel of his weapon trained on Sutton's chest. Behind him stands Allison, eyes wide, face pale.

Panic claws at my throat, and I scramble to my feet, swaying when my head throbs in protest.

"Steven," I say, but he doesn't even look at me.

My brother's eyes are wide as he darts glances from Sutton to the Sheriff's body on the ground at Suttons' feet. And I realize with horror what sort of assumptions he's making right now.

"Steven, it's not what it looks like," I say.

"Save it, Ser," he snaps. And then to Sutton, "You're under arrest—for murder."

KEEP READING WITH MIDNIGHT BOUND: THE incredible finale to Heather Hildenbrand's Mated by Midnight trilogy!

About Heather Hildenbrand

Heather Hildenbrand lives in coastal Virginia where she writes paranormal and urban fantasy romance with lots of kissing & killing. Her most frequent hobbies are truck camping with her goldendoodle, talking to her plants, and avoiding killer slugs.

You can find out more about Heather and her books at www.heatherhildenbrand.com, by subscribing to her Newsletter, or joining her Facebook reader group!

Also by Heather Hildenbrand

Dark Wolf Soul

Deadly Wolf Bite

Broken Wolf Heart

One Dark Spark

Two Blazing Hearts

Three Scorched Kingdoms

To Hunt A Wolf

To Kiss A Wolf

To Keep A Wolf

Wolf Cursed

Wolf Captive

Wolf Chosen

Wolf Revealed

A Witch's Call

A Witch's Destiny

A Witch's Fate

A Witch's Soul

A Witch's Prophecy

A Witch's Hope

Twisted Tides

The Girl Who Cried Werewolf

The Girl Who Cried Captive

The Girl Who Cried War

The Winter Witch

The Spring Witch

A Witch's Heart

Midnight Mate

Goddess Ascending

Goddess Claiming

Goddess Forging

Kiss of Death

Knock Em Dead

Death's Door

Dead to Rights

Dead End

The Girl Who Called The Stars

The Girl Who Ruled The Stars

Alpha Games

Alpha Trials

Alpha Chosen

Dirty Blood

Cold Blood

Blood Bond

Blood Rule

Broken Blood

One Hour: bonus novella

Imitation

Deviation

Generation

Guarded by the Alpha

Alpha Undercover

Mated to the Wilde Bear

The Bear's Fated Mate

Protected By the Bear

The Badge and the Bear

Tragic Ink: A Havenwood Falls story

Contemporary Romance as Violet Stafford

Stay For Summer

The Breakup Bet

Heather also writes contemporary romcom under the name Moxie Rose. Find out more about her books at moxierosebooks.com.

Quarantine Crush

Corporate Crush